Warning B
In His Head. H
Off-

He wasn't ready for any relationship, much less one with his employee. How many times had he reminded himself of that?

Joe stepped out of his car and leaned against it. "Thank you for following me home, Joe. It wasn't necessary, but I do appreciate it."

"Just wanted to make sure you got home safely, Ali."

She faced him and leaned over to give him a little kiss on his cheek. "That's sweet."

Sweet? Joe's hackles went up. He spread his legs and braced Ali's waist with his hands, pulling her closer. Her exotic scent went straight to his brain. "Can you forget that I'm your boss for one night?"

His gaze dropped down to the ripe fullness of her mouth.

Ali blinked. Then a beautiful smile emerged. "I think so. Why?"

Joe answered her by cupping a hand around her neck and bringing her mouth to his. "To show you I'm not that sweet," he whispered before he crushed his mouth to hers.

Dear Reader,

I have always loved fairy tales. *Cinderella* and *Beauty and the Beast* count among my favorites, so when I wrote Joe Carlino and Ali Pendrake's story it was with those two tales in mind.

Ali, the beautiful Cinderella, must transform into Plain Jane to catch the eye of the man she loves. Her "makeover in reverse" is fun to watch. You'll find yourself cheering Ali's last-ditch attempt to get her boss, hunky computer-genius Joe, to notice her.

Like the Beast in Disney's fairy tale, Joe doesn't know he wants love in his life. His vow to never engage in an office romance spurs Ali's clever plan to change his mind.

I hope you enjoy *Seduction on the CEO's Terms,* the second installment of Napa Valley Vows. Sit back, kick your shoes off and sip from a glass of great California wine.

Fall into the fantasy!

Happy reading,

Charlene

CHARLENE SANDS

SEDUCTION ON THE CEO'S TERMS

Silhouette Desire

Published by Silhouette Books

America's Publisher of Contemporary Romance

ISBN-13: 978-0-373-73040-7

Recycling programs for this product may not exist in your area.

SEDUCTION ON THE CEO'S TERMS

This edition published by arrangement with Harlequin Books S.A.

For questions and comments about the quality of this book please contact us at Customer_eCare@Harlequin.ca.

Visit Silhouette Books at www.eHarlequin.com

Printed in U.S.A.

Books by Charlene Sands

Silhouette Desire

The Heart of a Cowboy #1488
Expecting the Cowboy's Baby #1522
Like Lightning #1668
Heiress Beware #1729
Bunking Down with the Boss #1746
Fortune's Vengeful Groom #1783
Between the CEO's Sheets #1805
The Corporate Raider's Revenge #1848
**Five-Star Cowboy* #1889
**Do Not Disturb Until Christmas* #1906
**Reserved for the Tycoon* #1924
Texan's Wedding-Night Wager #1964
†Million-Dollar Marriage Merger #2016
†Seduction on the CEO's Terms #2027

*Suite Secrets
†Napa Valley Vows

CHARLENE SANDS

Award-winning author Charlene Sands writes bold, passionate, heart-stopping heroes and always…really good men! She's a lover of all things romantic, having married her high school sweetheart, Don. She is the proud recipient of the Readers' Choice Award and double recipient of the Booksellers Best Award, having written twenty-eight romances to date, both contemporary and historical Western. Charlene is a member of Romance Writers of America and belongs to the Orange County and Los Angeles Chapters of RWA where she volunteers as the Published Authors Liaison.

When not writing, she loves movie dates with her hubby, playing cards with her children, reading romance, great coffee, Pacific beaches, country music and anything chocolate. She also loves to hear from her readers. You can reach Charlene at www.charlenesands.com or P.O. Box 4883, West Hills, CA 91308. You can find her on eHarlequin's Silhouette Desire Blog and Facebook, too!

To Bill, Carol, Angi and Eric—the Petti.
Thanks for being my biggest fans and source of
love and support. I'm happy to call you family!
With special gratitude to my sister Carol
and brother-in-law Bill for making me an auntie!

One

Ali Pendrake sat at her desk at the Carlino Wines office, hitting the computer keys in rapid succession. She'd been at the top of her keyboarding class in college seven years ago, being not only a speedy typist but an accurate one. Today her usual tenacious focus waned and mistakes abounded.

"Darn it, Ali. You dummy," she muttered under her breath. She hit the backspace key and fixed her error, her concentration lost today.

Stealing a glance at her boss, Joe Carlino, Ali sighed. Joe's attention was glued to the computer screen in his executive office as he mumbled and crunched numbers. Deliberately, she'd positioned her desk in the outer office to afford herself this view of him.

No matter how hard she'd tried, she couldn't get Joe off her mind. Working alongside him in New York last year for a software giant, Ali had come to know him fairly well. Tall, dark-haired and extremely handsome behind the glasses he wore, Ali admired his intelligence, dedication and honest work ethic more than his good looks. He'd always treated her with respect, and Ali appreciated that.

Usually men took one look at her and discounted her intellect and ability. All they saw was a rather buxom auburn-haired woman with a pretty face and nice legs, so of course, she couldn't possibly have any brains. Most male employers had never given her a chance. Oh, they'd pretended to hire her for her capabilities, but all too soon harsh reality would set in when they made nonprofessional overtures.

The last thing Ali wanted was to be like her mother. Umpteen boyfriends and five husbands later, Justine Holcomb, a one-time beauty queen, gloried in the attentions of men. The former Miss Oklahoma never missed a chance to scope out wealthy, powerful men and manipulate them into marriage.

Ali only wanted *one* real good man. And that man wouldn't look at her twice.

"Ali, could you come in here?" When Joe popped his head out of his office, his thin black-rimmed glasses slipped down his nose Clark-Kent style.

Excitement buzzed within her at the sound of his voice. She'd never wanted her feelings for Joe to show. She'd enjoyed working with him in a professional manner in New York. It had been a rarity and an experience she'd valued. But then his father died, and he'd been called home to help run the family wine empire.

She'd driven him to LaGuardia Airport as her last official act as his personal assistant. He'd taken her in his arms and kissed her goodbye. Now memories of the exquisite press of his mouth on hers, his musky scent, the scratch of his day-old beard on her skin and the way he held her tight in his arms flashed through her mind. In that instant, everything inside her had gone hot; her body had oozed with desire. She'd looked up and met the gleam of desire in his eyes.

They'd stared at each other for a long time, saying nothing. She didn't know what to say. He'd obviously felt the same awkwardness in the situation after that kiss and had left her standing there pondering what had happened.

Since then, there wasn't a day that went by when she didn't think of him, and to her great surprise those thoughts weren't G-rated. In fact, her traitorous mind conjured up sexy images of Joe that stole her breath.

So when he'd called, offering her the opportunity to uproot her life and work to join him in northern California, the decision hadn't been difficult. She'd been ecstatic and jumped at the offer. She figured she'd have another chance with Joe. She happily left the Big Apple's rat race behind.

But after three weeks on the job, Ali was sure the potted plant in the corner of the room got more attention from Joe than she did. He was all business, pretending that the kiss they'd shared at the airport hadn't blown them both away. In truth, no man she'd met recently had been *less* interested in her.

"Sure, Joe. I'll be right in." She picked up her notepad, her BlackBerry and her wits and followed him into his office.

He waited for her to sit down before taking a seat behind his desk. His warm smile devastated her. "I realized that I haven't asked you how you're settling in here in Napa." He leaned back in his leather seat, waiting for her to reply.

"Just dandy, boss." She returned his smile. "It's different and all, but you know what they say, a girl's gotta do what a girl's gotta do."

Joe peered over his glasses at her. "How's that?"

She shrugged, and her white peasant blouse slipped off her shoulder. Joe didn't appear to notice when she adjusted it back into place, his focus staying on her face. "I like working with you," she said truthfully. "I'm glad to be here. I think we make a good team."

Joe nodded slowly. "I appreciate that. So you have no problems? No questions?"

Yes, you don't seem to know I'm alive.

"Not really. Not about work. I would love to learn more about the Napa area, though. I thought I'd start venturing out on the weekends."

"Sounds like a good plan."

She straightened her calf-length skirt. She'd gone for the gypsy look today. Hoop earrings and her bright auburn hair down in curls added some flavor to her outfit. She had smarts and was proud of her achievements, but she also loved fashion. Her flamboyant style often garnered compliments from the other Carlino Wines employees. If nothing else, it was an icebreaker and a way to meet people who had worked for the family for a long time.

Joe stared at her for a moment. She sat, waiting for him to voice the reason he'd called her into his office. Usually, it was to go over accounts, check monthly reports or give her an assignment. His silence made her wonder. "Is there anything I'm doing wrong?"

"Hell, no," Joe said. "You're the best employee we have on-site."

"Well, thank you."

"That's the reason I've asked you in here today. I, uh, well, I have a favor to ask. And I won't hold it against you if you can't help me out with this."

Ali waited for a moment before the suspense got to her. She gestured impatiently with both hands. "Spit it out, Joe."

He chuckled and shook his head.

She grinned.

"Okay, okay. I've offered to give Rena and Tony a wedding reception. You've met my brother and sister-in-law, right?"

"Great people," Ali said.

"It's a long story, but they got married secretly a short time ago, and well, now they want to renew their vows and have a reception."

"You offered to throw it for them?"

"More like my brother Nick roped me into it. What do I know about planning a party like that, right?"

She nodded.

"That's where you come in. I need your help. I'll understand if you're too busy to help me out with this—"

"Are you kidding?" Ali stood, excited at the prospect. "I love a good party. You won't have to ask me twice. What's the timetable on this?"

"Well, the sooner the better. Tony mentioned he wanted to do it ASAP. Say, in three weeks?"

"That's doable."

"Really?" Joe stood, too, an expression of relief washing over his features. "It may mean working together some weekends—that's if you're not too busy."

"I'm not too busy." *Was he joking?* She'd sat around her apartment at night bored to tears. Not that she couldn't have company, but the men who'd asked her out didn't compare to the computer brain—she refused to call Joe a geek—who seemed to occupy her mind lately.

"You might not have time to check out the sights around here."

Ali's mind clicked into high gear. "I'll make you a deal. If I help plan this successfully, then you can show me the sights in wine country. Fair is fair, Joe."

Joe adjusted the glasses on his nose, and Ali recognized that sign. Whenever Joe needed extra time to contemplate a question, he played with those glasses. "I can show you the inner workings of a computer better than I can be your Napa Valley tour guide."

"Joe," Ali said, refusing to let him off the hook, "you grew up here. You *know* this area." This was her opportunity to see Joe in less sterile surroundings. She really wanted to get to know him better. Her recent work relationship with Dwayne Hicks made her extremely wary of all men. Dwayne had exacted more from her than secretarial skills, and things had gotten ugly. Joe was the only man she'd trusted to take a chance with. And she really did love a good party. "Are we on?"

"I really appreciate this, Ali. Yes, we're on."

After returning to his office, Joe picked up his phone and dialed Nick's number. He reached him on the second ring.

"Hey, Joe. What's up?"

"Tony's wedding reception is in the works as we speak."

"That's good news. I knew you'd come through."

"Hey, not me. I'm not the wedding planner. I've got a one-woman task force, and I know she'll do a great job."

When his father died, his brother Tony had called both he and Nick home to honor the terms of Santo Carlino's will. All three sons were to take the helm at Carlino Wines for a period of six months and figure out which son would be better suited to run the family empire. It was his father's dying wish. Joe had left his life behind on the East Coast to help Tony and Nick, but he'd never have guessed part of his job description would be as a wedding planner.

Secretly, Tony had married his first love and high school

sweetheart, Rena Fairfield, shortly after her husband's death in order to save her winery and provide for her unborn child. After they fell back in love with each other, Rena had finally come around to letting their secret out. And Tony didn't trust anyone outside the family to see that his renewal of vows and reception were done right. He'd entrusted his brothers with the honor.

Joe sighed with relief. With Ali's help now, he knew it all would work out. She was always up for a challenge, and he had faith that she'd do a superb job.

"And you're going to come in on deadline with this?"

"Yeah, we'll be in the right time frame," Joe replied.

"You talked your gorgeous assistant into helping you, didn't you?"

"Nick." Joe sighed. "Her name is Ali Pendrake. And yes, she's taking on the project. We'll need a female's input, and she's very capable."

Nick chuckled. "So you've told me about a hundred times. Beauty and brains is a dynamite combo in a woman, Joe."

"I guess so," Joe said, fidgeting with his computer keyboard. He didn't like the direction this conversation was taking.

"So, you're *really* not interested in her?" Nick asked.

"No, of course not. She's my employee. I thought I made myself clear on that."

Joe dismissed the one time he'd held Ali in his arms and kissed her. His gesture of farewell at the New York airport that day had gotten a little out of control. But his emotions had been running high at the time. His father had just passed away, and he'd been called home. His life had changed drastically, and Ali was there for him, lending support and comfort. Kissing her had been impulsive—and so damn good that his head had spun.

He'd thought of her often after that. But after his assistant and ex-fiancée Sheila's betrayal, an office romance of any kind was out of the question. She had cut his heart out when she'd dumped him for another man. Joe had a will of iron, and though Ali was beautiful and had traits he admired, he knew he'd never pursue anything with her but a working relationship. He'd offered her the job in Napa only because he knew he could work beside her and not get emotionally involved. It was hard for both of his brothers to understand that he just simply didn't see Ali that way.

"So, you wouldn't mind if I asked her out?" Nick questioned.

Joe furrowed his brows. He hadn't seen this coming. Nick had his fair share of women. He wasn't one to spend his nights alone. But Ali and *Nick?* Joe couldn't picture them together. His jaw clenched, and he contemplated for a moment.

"Joe? Did you hear me?"

"I heard you, little brother."

"We've never stepped on each other's toes when it came to women, but if you're clearly not interested in Ali—"

"I'm not."

"So, I can ask her out without causing you sleepless nights?"

"No, you can't ask her out."

"I can't?" Nick didn't sound too upset. "Why?"

"No offense, but I wouldn't subject any of my employees to dating you, especially Ali. You'd likely break her heart. And then she'd leave town, and I'd be out one damn good personal assistant."

"You don't give me much credit."

"History doesn't lie."

"Maybe I'm a changed man."

"Maybe…but I don't want you to use one of my employees as your test subject."

Nick laughed. "Man, you really don't have a good opinion of me, do you?"

"In any other arena, you're a great guy. Just *not* when it comes to women." Joe was ready to leave this subject behind. "So when are you leaving for Europe?"

"In a few days. But have no fear, I'll be back in time for the big hoopla. I wouldn't miss Tony's wedding reception."

"Yeah, your timing is impeccable. Leaving me to deal with all the details, while you're off—"

"Selling wine, schmoozing with customers and making sure Carlino Wines stays on top."

"Among other things," Joe muttered.

In truth, it bothered him how glad he was that Nick would be out of the picture for a couple of weeks. If he wasn't around, he couldn't be romancing Ali. In his analytical mind, that shouldn't be a factor. But he was damn glad of it just the same.

"I'll see you at home tonight," Nick said.

"I'll be working late with Ali."

"Hey, I can't blame you, bro." Joe visualized his brother's smirk. "Regardless of all your denials."

Joe hung up the phone and shook his head.

Ali came in then, holding a calendar in her hands. "Joe, I think we'd better set a date for the wedding reception."

Ali's darn blouse had slipped down again, and it was all he could do to keep from staring at her soft shoulder. She had such beautiful creamy skin. He'd have to be blind not to notice.

Every day with Ali was a fashion extravaganza. Today she looked like a gypsy princess—a very sexy, approachable one. He'd never noticed her style much in New York, but now, Nick and Tony's prodding was making it hard for him to *keep* from noticing her.

But the more he noticed, the more he was determined to keep her off-limits. She wasn't his type of woman anyway. She reminded him too much of Sheila with her quick wit, flamboyant nature and sense of adventure. He'd been playing with fire in his office relationship with Sheila, and he wasn't about to jump back into the flames anytime soon. A broken engagement and being left for a flashy billionaire wasn't his idea of a good time. Joe had been smacked down by that betrayal, and he had no intention of bounding up on the ten count to take another knockout punch.

"I think that's a good idea. Sit down, and we'll go over some dates. Then I'll check with Tony to make sure it'll work for them."

"I'm already on it. I just spoke with Rena. She's coming into town today, and we're having lunch. I'll cross-check the dates with her once you and I come up with something feasible."

Joe smiled and leaned back in his seat. He wasn't sorry he'd asked Ali to come work for him. Time and again, she'd proven to him that hiring her was the smartest thing he'd ever done. "I'm glad you took me up on my offer to come to Napa, Ali."

Ali's jade-green eyes lit up. "You are?"

"Yeah, you're in line for employee of the year."

Ali's gaze dropped to the calendar in her hands. "How nice."

Joe drew his brows together. Ali wasn't thrilled with his pronouncement. Somehow he'd disappointed her, but he couldn't figure out how. If anyone understood an honest work ethic, it was Ali Pendrake.

He thought she'd be happy that he'd recognized her many capabilities.

Rena Carlino was beautifully pregnant. The minute she walked into the office, Ali noticed the bright beam of happiness on her face and the lightness in her step despite sporting a rounded belly.

From all she'd gathered from Joe, Rena hadn't had an easy life and Tony had caused most of her trouble. The former race car champion had left Rena in the dust years ago to pursue his dream of racing stock cars. Jilted and heartbroken, Rena had married David Montgomery, Tony's best friend. She'd come to blame Tony for David's untimely death, faulting him for her heartache and the terrible things done to ruin her family's winery.

But when Tony returned to Napa twelve years later and honored the vow he made to Rena's dying husband to marry his pregnant wife, their rocky road had smoothed out. To his credit, Tony had come through in the end. Now, Tony loved both mother-to-be and baby and the evidence of that love beamed in Rena's eyes.

"Hi, Ali."

Ali stood and smiled. "Hi." She walked around the desk to embrace Rena. "You look fabulous."

Rena rubbed her belly and grinned. "Thank you. Most days, I'd disagree with you. But I made an extra effort today, since I was meeting you for lunch."

"I don't believe that for a minute."

"Oh, believe it. I feel *fine,* it's just that I'm moving so much slower these days. I'm used to doing a lot of work. I was always up early, working hard at the winery, but now things have slowed down. It's to be expected. And Tony is so protective that he won't let me lift anything heavier than my purse."

Ali chuckled, and a slight wave of envy coursed through her system. Tony adored Rena, and Ali wondered when her time would come to feel that same sort of love from a man. "I hear the baby's healthy as a horse."

"Yes, and I plan to keep it that way. Did you hear we're having a boy?"

"Oh Lord, love him. Another male Carlino in the world? I feel sorry for the next generation of baby girls."

Rena grinned. "I know what you mean. The Carlino men are a handful. I guess I'll have my work cut out for me."

Ali really admired Rena. She'd been given a lot to deal with lately, and she'd taken it all in stride. She'd finally come to accept the role as Tony's wife without giving up her own dream of saving her family's legacy, Purple Fields Winery. But even more amazing was that she'd forgiven Tony for all the hurt he'd caused and accepted him as the father of her child.

Ali grabbed her knockoff Gucci handbag and her briefcase. "Excuse me a second. I'll just let Joe know we're leaving for lunch." Ali turned and bumped smack into Joe, stepping on his toes and bumping heads. "Oh!"

Joe grabbed her arms to steady her, his touch sending lightning bolts straight through her. She was so close to him that their breaths mingled. The subtle scent of Hugo cologne was heaven to her senses.

"Are you okay?" he asked with concern.

Ali stared at him and nodded. "I didn't see you. That's what you get for sneaking up on me."

"I wasn't sneak—" But he stopped when he noticed her smile.

"I'm fine, Joe," she said. "You?"

Joe straightened. For a computer whiz, Joe didn't have an ounce of jelly on his body. He was granite hard, but rather than speculate, Ali would like firsthand knowledge. *If only...*

Joe dropped his hands from her arms, blinked and then took a step back. "I'll let you know if I develop a headache later."

"I'm really sorr—" Then Ali stopped when she realized Joe was joking, something he rarely did.

He walked around her to give Rena a hug. "Hi, sister-in-law. How's my brother treating you?"

Rena sighed. "Like a queen. I've got no complaints, Joe. And I can't thank both of you enough for taking on the wedding details. I'm afraid with all the construction we're doing to the house now it's a bit much for Tony and me."

"No problem," Joe said. "With Ali's help, it should run like clockwork." Joe glanced her way, and her heart did a little flip.

"You're welcome to join us for lunch, Joe," Rena said, "but I'll warn you, we'll be talking wedding and baby, and there's no getting around it."

Fear entered his eyes for a moment. "I'll leave you two to hash out the details. Once you have a plan, then I'll chime in. Thanks, anyway."

"Sure, Joe." Rena glanced at Ali and they both giggled.

"What's so funny?"

"Having three root canals without anesthesia sounds better to you than having lunch with us today. Admit it, boss."

Joe shrugged his shoulders in feigned innocence, which made him look sexier than all get-out. "Have a nice lunch, ladies."

They bid him farewell, and twenty minutes later after a nice walk along the main street of town, they were seated at an outside café that served sandwiches, salads and specialty coffees.

Ali ordered a double vanilla latte, while Rena opted for a glass of cranberry juice. They sipped their drinks while waiting for the salads they'd ordered.

"So how do you like Napa?" Rena asked.

"From what I can tell, I like it. It's a far cry from New York."

"Did you grow up there?"

She shook her head. "Heavens, no. I'm a southern gal from Oklahoma originally. My mama and daddy divorced when I was just a kid. Seems Mama wanted a better life for us, and Daddy just wasn't up for the task. She was Miss Oklahoma after all and figured she deserved better than a man who worked for the county as a deputy sheriff. As soon as she could, she moved us to the East Coast. I grew up in a string of big cities from Boston to New York. We never really settled anywhere for long."

"Sounds like you had it tough as a kid."

She shrugged. "It is what it is. I still keep in touch with my dad. He's remarried now and perfectly happy and still working in law enforcement."

"And your mom? Do you see her?"

"We see each other whenever we can." Ali wouldn't tell Rena her mother was on husband number five now. Ali had been bounced around from one household to another, from city to city, her mother never finding satisfaction in the men she married. She'd always wanted to elevate herself and thought money and power would be the ticket. Now, she was married to a millionaire attorney with political ties. "My mama leads a very busy social life." Ali shook her head and shuddered. "That life's not for me. So yeah, Napa's a nice change of pace."

"I wondered why you'd agree to uproot your life to work here…for Joe." Rena's brows raised, and her blue eyes beamed with clarity. "Can I ask you a personal question?"

Ali nodded.

"Are you and Joe…"

She shook her head. "Nothing."

"Really?" Rena sounded truly puzzled. "Because I swear, I thought I saw sparks between you two at the office."

"That's just me being me. Joe isn't interested."

Rena opened her mouth to reply but then clammed up.

"Were you going to say something?"

Rena stared at her for a moment. "No, it's not my place."

Darn it. "I understand," Ali said.

Ali opened her briefcase and took out her calendar. "Shall we set a date for the big occasion?"

"Sure," Rena said, and leaned over to glance at the calendar.

They settled on a Saturday three weeks away. The celebration would be held on the Carlino estate, the renewal of vows under an arbor of flowers in the backyard and the reception on the grounds.

"I'm doing this for Tony," Rena said. "For years, I wouldn't step foot on Carlino land. This is one way for me to show Tony that I've truly let the past go."

"You're very lucky to have this second chance, Rena." Ali cast her a small smile, suddenly feeling that life was passing her by.

Rena reached over and took her hand. "If I've learned one thing about life it's that you've got to make the best out of every moment and go after what you want." She lowered her voice. "If you have a goal in mind, don't let anything stop you."

Ali blinked. It was a lightbulb moment for her. She'd never been a quitter. Joe Carlino had enticed her to come to Napa, and she'd jumped at the chance because she cared about him. Ali wasn't one to wait around for things to happen.

If Joe needed a little push, then Ali wouldn't mind giving her sexy employer a shove in the right direction.

Two

As soon as Ali opened her front door, Joe realized his mistake in coming to her apartment tonight.

"Hi, Joe." She beamed him a smile. "I can't thank you enough for coming by. I'm in computer hell at the moment. Your timing is perfect, I just finished my Pilates workout."

He'd *noticed.* She wore spandex, a tight midriff top that pushed her cleavage to its limits and black pants that hugged her tiny waist. A glittering sheen of moisture coated her exposed skin.

Damn Nick and his constant jabbing. Joe didn't want to notice Ali as anything but his assistant. Feeling beholden to help when she'd complained about her computer problems today, he'd offered to stop by to look at it. "Happy to help out, Ali."

She stepped aside to let him in as she sipped from an Arrowhead water bottle. "I don't know what happened to it. Like I explained at the office, it just froze up on me. But I'm glad you came by anyway. You've never seen my apartment."

"River Ridge has a great reputation," Joe said. He'd gone out of his way to find her a good location that suited her when she'd accepted the job.

"It's a great place. I've always wanted a fireplace. I love the view from my living room window, too. Come take a look," she offered, and walked over to a wide picture window overlooking a garden setting. "There's a little pond out there. Can you see it?"

Joe stepped beside her and gazed out the window, indulging her. He'd made sure she'd gotten an apartment with the best view. He'd checked out this apartment before Ali had moved in. Adjusting the glasses on his nose, he narrowed his eyes. "I see two ducks splashing around."

"Let me see," Ali said, brushing up against him. "Oh, how sweet."

Her joy at such a little pleasure touched him. Joe stepped away from the window. "Different from living in New York, isn't it?"

"That's an understatement," she said with a groan. Then she sipped her water again. "Well, I'd better get showered and changed. I'll show you my computer, and maybe you can work your magic while I'm cleaning up. Can I get you anything?"

Joe kept his focus on her face and shook his head. "No, I'm good." He wouldn't allow his mind to conjure up images of her showering.

"Okay, then follow me." She walked down a short hallway. "This is my bedroom," she said, pointing and continuing to move.

Joe caught a glimpse of soft yellow hues, a large inviting bed and mismatched furniture that somehow looked perfect together. A fresh scent of lavender emanated from the room.

He followed her into a smaller bedroom down the hall. "I haven't fixed it up yet. It's sort of my office, slash, junk room, slash, guest room."

Joe scanned the room. "It's not very messy."

"You haven't seen what's stashed in the closet." She grinned.

"Shoved everything in there, did you?"

"*And* under the bed."

"All this to impress me?"

"Well, I didn't want you to see how unorganized this room is. I have a rep to protect, you know."

Joe shook his head in amusement.

"Okay, boss. I'll get out of your hair now. Just twitch your nose and fix the darn thing."

"I'll try."

Ali turned to exit the room and offered as a parting shot, "If you can't fix it, nobody can."

Joe grinned. He appreciated the compliment. Joe was good with computers and had been fascinated with them since he was a young boy. While all the other kids were involved in sports or getting into mischief, Joe stayed at home, learning the intricacies of the newest form of technology. He'd never felt he'd missed out on his childhood, though his father would often look in on him in his bedroom and frown.

Fifteen minutes later with the computer problem solved, Joe strode out of the office/junk room/guest room and walked down the hallway, passing Ali's bedroom. The door was closed, the shower had stopped and a vision of Ali towel-drying her naked body entered his mind.

His will of iron allowed him only two seconds to enjoy that image before he proceeded to the living room. He sat down on the sofa, picked up a *People* magazine then flipped through the pages. When the doorbell rang, Joe stood, glancing at Ali's room down the hallway.

"Ali," a male voice carried through the doorway. "It's Royce. And I have something for you I think you're going to like."

Joe stared at the door for a moment. When Ali didn't come out of her room to answer it, Joe walked over and yanked the door open.

A man wearing oven mitts holding a casserole dish raised his eyebrows. "Sorry, I didn't know Ali had company. I'm Royce."

"Joe."

The shaggy blond-haired Brad Pitt lookalike didn't seem happy to find Joe in Ali's apartment. And Joe didn't make it easy on him.

"I'm Ali's neighbor."

Joe nodded.

"I brought her my newest creation. Ali tests out some of my meals for me."

Joe narrowed his eyes. "Hold on. I'll get Ali."

"I'm here," Ali said, coming into the room dressed in jeans and a white knit top, still towel-drying her gorgeous auburn hair. As she whizzed by him, he caught the scent of fresh citrus. "Oh, hi, Royce. What did you bring me this time?"

Royce seemed relieved to see her. "Champagne chicken with a touch of cognac."

"Yum. Smells great. Come in and set it down on the stove. Joe, this is Royce, my neighbor. He's a chef at Cordial Contessa. Royce, this is my…uh, Joe."

"We've just met," Joe said, watching how Royce's gaze fixed on Ali. "Ali works for me at Carlino Wines," Joe said.

Ali furrowed her brows and stared at the two of them. "Well, thanks, Royce. I'll give you my review of your latest creation tomorrow. Unless you want to join us?"

"Join you? What are you two doing?"

Ali looked his way. "Joe's a computer genius. He's fixing my senior-citizen computer. Poor thing is on its last legs."

"*Fixed* your computer," Joe corrected.

"You fixed it already?" Ali's eyes lit up, and Joe took immense satisfaction in her reaction. "There, you see," she turned to Royce. "He *is* a genius."

Ali returned her attention to Joe, her green eyes round and bright. "Thank you so much."

"No problem. Your computer has a lot of life left in it. You just need to upgrade a few things." Joe took the list he'd jotted down out of his pocket and handed it to her.

Ali's smile faded when she glanced at the items he'd listed. "Okay."

Joe gently grabbed the list from her hand. "You know what, I'll take care of it for you."

"Really? But you've already—"

"It's not a problem, Ali. Consider it payback for helping me with the wedding."

"The wedding?" Royce interrupted, casting Ali a curious look.

"Joe's brother is getting married, and he needs a little help with the planning."

"Is that part of your job description?" Royce asked with a disingenuous smile, directing his attention solely to Ali.

"She's doing this off-the-clock, as a favor to me. Not that it's any of your business," Joe said.

Ali intervened, appearing a little nervous. "I'm happy

to do it. I love planning fun events. I know parties the way Joe knows computers."

Joe met Royce with a hard stare. Who the hell was this guy anyway? Why was he so damn protective of Ali? He tested Joe's even-keeled temper in the span of just a few minutes.

Ali placed her hand on Royce's arm and guided him toward the door. "Thanks for the champagne chicken, Royce."

"Anytime, Ali," he said. "Let me know what you think."

"I will," she said, closing the door behind him.

Joe walked up to her. "Is he your boyfriend?"

Ali shook her head. "No."

"Gay?"

She laughed. "Hardly."

From her laughter and the surprised expression on her face, Joe surmised Royce had ulterior motives for bringing Ali his latest culinary creation.

"I think he's just a little protective of me."

"You think?" Joe asked between tight lips.

She shrugged. "I've confided in him about some things in my past, and well now, I think I shouldn't have."

What sort of things? Joe had been work-close to Ali, but they'd never confided in personal matters before. He felt a twinge of jealousy that shouldn't be. But still, it gnawed at him all the same.

"He's interested in you, Ali," Joe said with blunt honesty.

"I've made it clear that we're just friends."

Hell, men never took that "just friends" garbage seriously. If they were interested in a woman, eventually it would come out.

Ali walked over to him and stared straight into his eyes.

Her fresh scent surrounded him. Her hair had dried in curls around her pretty face. She glanced at his mouth, and Joe had a difficult time keeping his focus. If she made another move toward him, he didn't think he'd stop her. And that could spell disaster.

He reminded himself that office romances never worked out. An image of Sheila flashed in his mind. He and his bright, feisty, flamboyant onetime fiancée were complete opposites. It had taken months to realize that marrying her would have been a big mistake.

"Can we forget about Royce?" Ali asked. "We have work to do on the wedding."

"Right, the wedding." Joe pushed his glasses farther up his nose and nodded. "Royce who?"

Ali went to bed that night thinking of Joe. For once, she noticed a chink in his armor. He'd actually seemed perturbed with Royce showing up. She could only find a bit of hope in that.

Royce had offered friendship when she'd first moved into River Ridge. He'd helped her settle in and was always around if she'd needed anything. After a couple of weeks, he began asking her out, but Ali had always made it clear that she wasn't looking for a relationship.

Royce had backed off and offered his understanding. He'd been so compassionate, and one night over a bottle of zin and his delicious shrimp scampi à la Contessa, Ali had confided in him about her past history. She'd explained about her tumultuous childhood with her mother and her latest office fiasco with her employer, Dwayne Hicks, a man who'd hired her under false pretenses, pursuing her sexually and giving her grief at the office because she'd denied him.

She'd filed harassment charges against him, and the

whole ordeal had left her somewhat scarred. No matter the right or wrong of it, lawsuits against employers didn't build great resumes.

That's why working for Joe Carlino had appealed to her. He'd been flawless as a boss and seemed to have no other agenda. Working alongside him, her feelings had grown out of respect and admiration.

Ali snuggled deeper into her bed. Joe was becoming more and more important in her life. Instead of fearing those feelings, she welcomed them with her whole heart. He was the only man on her radar, and she wished they'd met outside of the office environment. They'd had a strictly professional working relationship. Until he'd kissed her at the airport, Ali held no hope for a relationship with him. But after that kiss—and if she'd read his jealousy right tonight—all was not lost.

The sun shone warm and bright into her apartment when Ali rose from bed the next morning. The Napa news report called for record-high temperatures today. With that in mind, Ali slipped on a sleeveless white eyelet sundress, tied it at the waist with a red leather belt, added beaded red jewelry around her neck and wrists and tucked her feet into matching three-inch sandals.

After a quick slurp of orange juice, Ali set out for the Carlino estate for her morning meeting with Joe. If she was going to plan a renewal of vows and a reception at the estate, she needed to see the house and grounds. When she'd come up with the idea last night, Joe hadn't balked. Always logical, Joe saw the value in her visit.

After being buzzed inside the gates, Ali drove up the stone driveway and parked the car. The estate and well-groomed grounds were massive, and the colorful rolling vineyards beyond lent a beautiful backdrop for the house.

A housekeeper named Carlotta met her outside the arched Mediterranean-style breezeway and showed her inside the house. She found herself face-to-face with Nick Carlino, who'd just descended the stairs. "Hey, Ali."

"Hi, Nick."

"You're here early. Joe said you'd be coming over for a meeting." He cast her an assessing look. "You look beautiful today."

"Thank you."

"What's the meeting about?" he asked.

"We're going over plans for the wedding before our real workday begins."

"Joe would be lost without you." He eased into a smile. "He really relies on you, doesn't he?"

"I guess so."

"He's always singing your praises to anyone who's willing to listen."

"And is that all he says about me?" The question slipped out much to her surprise "Sorry, I shouldn't have asked you that."

"No need to apologize. As far as I'm concerned, Joe's got rocks in his head." Nick winked. "Come on, I'll take you to him."

Nick led her outside to a covered stone deck overlooking a swimming pool that blended into the landscape so well it appeared born of the earth rather than man-made.

"Joe does laps in the pool every day. Clears his mind for all the numbers he crunches," Nick explained.

Ali spotted Joe gliding through the pool. Sleek and well-muscled, Joe dipped in and out of the smooth blue waters, and Ali's heart swelled.

"Hey, Joe. You have company," Nick called out. He

turned to Ali. "Unfortunately, I've got a plane to catch. Thanks for helping Joe out. He needs it." Again, Nick winked, and before he turned to walk away, he offered one last parting comment. "Just so you know, my brother isn't as noble as he seems."

"Meaning?"

"Don't give up on him."

Ali opened her mouth in denial, but Nick's astute look spoke of the futility in that. He wouldn't buy it, and Ali wasn't all too sure she could sell it to him.

Oh God, was she that obvious?

"I'll be right there," Joe called to her from the far end of the pool.

Joe bounded out of the pool, and she caught her first real glimpse of another side of Joe—the stunning, well-built, tanned and gorgeous man who looked as if he could conquer an enemy in one fell swoop.

Ali's throat constricted.

Her Clark Kent had just transformed into Superman.

Three

Morning sunshine cast a golden sheen over Joe's entire body as he stood by the pool's edge. Water dripped from his hair to his shoulders and then slowly drizzled down his rock-hard torso. She could compare him to a Greek god, but nothing topped Superman in her estimation.

She watched him towel off, then throw his arms into a shirt and head her way. Ali got a grip real fast. She couldn't be caught drooling.

"Sorry," he said as he approached. "I didn't realize the time."

"How many laps do you do?"

"One hundred."

Her mouth gaped open. "One hundred? Every day?"

"Just about."

"No wonder."

"No wonder what?" He looked puzzled.

Ali had to learn to stop thinking out loud. "Oh, um. I

was thinking about your stamina…you must have great stamina."

Joe smiled. "I've built it up over the years." He walked over to a large inlaid stone and iron patio table and picked up his glasses. Taking a second to clean them with the end of his shirt, he narrowed his eyes. "So what do you think?"

"About your stamina? Very impressive."

"No," he said, running a hand through his hair. He put his glasses on, and this was the Joe Ali had come to know. "I mean, about using this place for the wedding."

"Are you kidding? It's a girl's dream come true, Joe. Your home is amazing, and I've only seen a small part of it."

"I'll rectify that in a few minutes. First let me shower and change. In the meantime, have a cup of coffee. I cooked you up some breakfast to have during our meeting."

"You cook, too?" Ali couldn't believe Joe had culinary skills, as well as his other talents.

"I get by. After my father died, our longtime cook retired, and we just never replaced her. Tony's living at Purple Fields now, and Nick and I are rarely home."

Joe walked over to a coffeepot on the patio counter. "What'll you have?"

"I'll get it, Joe. Don't worry about me."

"Okay, I'll be back in five, then I'll give you the grand tour."

Ali watched him leave, her heart in her throat. She couldn't fight her feelings any longer. All shreds of rationality escaped her. She'd never before met a man like Joe Carlino. Before, she'd welcomed the challenge to get him interested in her. But now, it went deeper than that. She admired Joe, found him unique and intelligent and sexy as sin. Emotions washed over as a question entered her mind.

Could she be falling in love with her boss?

"I think your home will work out nicely," Ali said after a cup of coffee and not-half-bad eggs Benedict. Joe cooked like he did everything else, with honed precision and accuracy.

She sat at the patio table after he'd given her the grand tour of his home. Stunning was an understatement. Joe's mother must have had a hand in decorating the house. He'd always spoken so fondly of her sweet, calming ways, and her talent for making a house a home was evident everywhere.

The entire home, though updated with modern conveniences, oozed warmth and love, giving off a Mediterranean flair from the polished carved wood furniture and colorful sofas to the pale golden walls and inlaid stone flooring.

Where the first floor was set to bring in the harmony of the family, the upstairs was laid out to accommodate privacy, each wing being a home within a home. The parents and three sons could enjoy their private suites and never bump into one another.

Silly, but Ali pictured herself here with Joe, living in the east wing of the house. It wasn't the grandeur that appealed to her but the sense of stability. Seeing Joe's brothers interact with each other—witnessing their family ties—had touched a sentimental chord within her.

She'd never had a real place to call home.

She fought her resentment tooth and nail, yet Ali couldn't forgive her mother for her lifestyle. She'd dragged her young child from town to town, marrying men who'd look upon Ali as a burden. At least, she'd always felt like a necessary evil that Justine's husbands had to endure.

Ali had inherited her mother's feisty, bubbly nature. She wasn't shy by any means. But unlike her mother, Ali had a career that she enjoyed. She'd worked hard for everything she'd achieved in life including her bachelor's degree in business. She had brains, thank goodness, and liked to use them.

But now, she was at a complete loss with her strong feelings for Joe. She'd never been in love before and wondered if the impeding sense of dread and earth-shattering excitement she felt was normal. The conflicting mix of emotions put her on unsteady ground.

And other than that one kiss, he really hadn't laid a hand on her. She'd never want to resort to her mother's means for snaring a man, and therein was her problem.

"Where should we hold the renewal of vows?" Joe asked, his focus and those dark piercing eyes intent on her. He'd changed from his swim trunks to black casual trousers and a white button-down shirt. Joe the Hunk had changed back into Joe the Boss.

She came out of her stupor to reply to his question. "Poolside. I think that'll be perfect," she said, the notion in her mind gaining momentum. "The sound of the rock waterfall and the glistening water below will be a great backdrop. We'll have a flower archway made for them to say their vows underneath but nothing too elaborate. The grounds are enough."

Joe looked out at the pool, giving a nod of agreement. "I think you're right."

"I'm always right," she teased.

"I know." Joe didn't blink as he shot back his response.

Ali stared into his eyes. Did he really have that much

faith in her abilities? "I think Rena will be pleased with what I have in mind. Do you think Tony will like my ideas?"

"Without a doubt. He has the woman he loves. That's all he cares about."

"I wish," Ali began, then bit down on her bottom lip.

"What do you wish?" Joe asked, touching a finger to his glasses. Ali knew his gestures and that one meant true curiosity. She couldn't relay her innermost wish, but she could turn the tables on him.

"Have you ever been in love, Joe?"

He blinked and shot his head back in surprise. "Me?"

She held her breath and nodded.

Joe pursed his lips and answered in a clipped tone. "Once. It didn't work out."

Ali was floored by his admission. He was a gorgeous, thirtysomething man who had a lot going for him, but somehow she couldn't picture Joe being in love.

Unless of course, it's with you, Ali.

"I'm sorry."

"Don't be," he said. "It was for the best." He dismissed the subject by flipping through a batch of menus she'd brought with her. "Now, what about the reception? Any ideas?"

"I have a few thoughts on the subject."

He nodded. "Good."

Ali stood and walked around the grounds, conjuring up images of how to best use the backyard and surrounding vineyards for the reception. But more so, she had to move away from her sexy boss to come to grips with the fact that Joe had been in love once. And maybe, he was holding on to that love. Maybe that's why he'd kept his distance. A knot twisted in the pit of her stomach.

Joe came up behind her. His nearness made her heart pound against her ribs. "What's your plan, Ali?"

In the world-according-to-Joe, you always had to have a plan.

Ali turned to find him close enough to touch. She searched his eyes, dying to know the truth. Ali made a decision right then and there to go for broke. "I'm working on it. But you can be sure when I come up with a good plan that you'll be the first to know."

Ali stood in the wine-tasting room at Purple Fields, browsing through the items on the shelves. The quaint shop spoke of decades of winemaking, a family legacy that Tony Carlino had a hand in saving.

Ali looked out of the shop's window to view the construction crew outside. It appeared every effort was being made to update the house without losing its original rustic style.

"Hello, Ali. This is a pleasant surprise."

Ali turned to face Rena, who had walked in from the backroom. "Hi," Ali said. "I hope you don't mind me stopping by."

"Not at all." Rena walked over to her. "It's good to see you again. Sorry about the mess outside. Tony needed more space. And with the baby coming, we thought it best to do the construction before he's born. Tony wanted to add a playroom for the baby, an office for himself and a full remodel of the kitchen for me."

"Wow! All that will be done before your little bambino enters the world?"

Rena nodded. "Carlinos have a way of making things happen."

Ali glanced out the window again and sighed. "If they want something badly enough I suppose."

Rena stared at her, furrowing her brows. "Ali, is something wrong?"

She shook her head. "No." She plastered on a big smile. "I came to give you an update on the wedding plans."

"Wonderful. I'm getting excited about it. Come, have a seat and let's talk."

Rena guided her to one of the three small round tables set in the corner portion of the room. "I'll get us something to drink first. Grape juice for me and our best merlot for you."

Rena returned shortly, handing her a wineglass. Ali sipped from it. "This is fabulous." She set the glass down on the cheery cornflower blue-and-white tablecloth and waited for Rena to take her seat. "Thank you."

"I should be thanking you for all you're doing. I hope Joe isn't working you too hard on this."

"Not at all. I, uh, listen, Rena, I have a confession to make," Ali said. She was never good at fibbing. "I could have called you with the update. We're just beginning with the plans, and there's not much to tell."

"Okay," Rena said, looking a little confused. "But you don't need a reason to stop by to say hello. You're new to Napa, and I'm happy to be your—"

"I do have a specific reason for coming here. Dang it, I'm so confused, and now I'm confusing you!"

Rena chuckled. "Ali, just tell me."

Ali chewed on her lower lip and took a deep breath. She was never one to hesitate about anything. "Okay, I think I'm in love with Joe," she finally blurted out.

Rena's eyes snapped wide-open. "Oh, wow."

"Yeah, wow. It's wonderful and terrifying."

Rena smiled and nodded in full agreement. "I know. That's exactly how I felt about Tony. I didn't want to love him, but those feelings just creep up on you and there's no denying them."

"Joe doesn't suspect anything. He barely knows I'm alive."

"Joe's involved in his work, but he knows you're alive, Ali. I can guarantee it."

"Yeah, I'm nominated for employee of the year."

Rena's smile faded and she cast her a solemn look. "You're serious about this? About him?"

"Very. I've never been in love before. I think Joe's perfect for me. Unfortunately, the only sheets he's interested in me slipping between are the Carlino Wine's tally sheets."

A chuckle burst from Rena's lips. "Sorry. You do have a way with words, Ali."

"It's a curse. I spit out exactly what I'm thinking."

"But not in a demeaning way. You're honest, and that's refreshing."

"Do you think I scare Joe?"

Rena thought about it a few seconds, and Ali was sorry she asked. Perhaps, she didn't want to know the answer to her question.

"No, it's not that," Rena said finally. "I know you don't frighten Joe. He may be a computer geek, but women don't intimidate him. In case you haven't noticed, beyond those brains, Joe's quite a hunk."

"Oh, I've noticed. But that's not the reason I think I love him."

Ali went on to explain to Rena that her reasons for loving Joe went way beyond his sexy good looks. What she'd noticed about him first and foremost was that he'd always taken her seriously, respecting her intelligence, treating her as an equal and *not* coming on to her five minutes after she'd been hired. Ali explained about her former employer. For all intents and purposes, she'd never thought she'd ever get involved with someone in the workplace, much less her boss. But she and Joe had a unique work relationship.

"I flat-out asked him if he's ever been in love, and he told me that he had, once. He didn't want to talk about it. Do you think he's still in love with her?"

"No," Rena said adamantly, bringing hope to her heart. "He's been over Sheila Maxwell for quite some time."

"So what is it?"

"Well, I can tell you this. Joe was burned really badly. Apparently, he became engaged to Sheila while she worked for him at Global Software. She was very beautiful and clever, from what I've been told. Joe thought the sun rose and set on her shoulders. His millions hadn't been enough for her. As you know, of all the Carlino men, Joe is the least flashy. He drives a hybrid car, wears conservative clothes and doesn't have a pretentious bone in his body.

"It wasn't enough for Sheila, though. As soon as an oilman from Texas with billions became interested in her, she dumped Joe like a hot potato."

"How awful for him."

"He didn't take it well. He felt duped and foolish for falling for her. I think Joe is just a little gun-shy right now. And for the record, Ali, he's vowed to never get involved with someone who works for him ever again."

Ali put her head down. "I get it now."

"Well, that's the bad news. The good news is that I think Joe is way off on this. If the right woman comes along—no matter where, when or how—he should act on it. I think he's interested in you, but he's holding on to the promise he made to himself."

"Nick told me Joe's not as noble as he seems. Maybe that's what he meant?"

"Maybe. You're a beautiful woman, Ali. You have flair and style, and if you don't mind me saying, you're sassy. I think Joe looks at you and warning bells go off in his head that scream, 'Stop!'"

"Wonderful," Ali said, feeling hopeless.

"All is not lost. Nick told me he wanted to ask you out, and Joe wouldn't hear of it. Joe was pretty adamant about it."

Ali's antenna went back up. "Did he say why?"

"Something about not wanting Nick to break your heart, but I think it's more than that. I think Joe was jealous."

"That's something," Ali acknowledged. She sipped her merlot, contemplating. "But what can I do about it other than jump his bones?"

Rena shook her head. "I think the opposite approach would work much better. We've got to remove that stop sign in his head. You've got to tone down your appearance and become less of a threat in his mind."

"You mean, a makeover in reverse?"

Rena smiled. "That's one way to put it. But yes, he may notice you more, if you're not on his mental do-not-touch list. Sort of like Cinderella turning back into a plain Jane."

Blood surged through her veins as Ali mulled the idea over. "I think it might work. I'm ready to try anything at this point."

"Trust me, Ali. If I didn't see sparks between you, I wouldn't encourage this. But Joe's a great guy and deserves love in his life again," Rena said, daring Ali with the gleam in her eyes.

"Nothing I've been doing so far has worked."

"If you decide to do this, I'll help in any way I can."

"Hah, so *Ali,* has an *ally.* Okay, I'll do it. If I succeed, I'll name our firstborn after you."

"And I'll hold you to that."

"When should this all happen?" Ali asked.

"Well, I think you should make a few subtle changes during the next few weeks."

"Like toning down my hair and makeup and my sass mouth?"

Rena shook her head with laughter. "Yes, but slowly. The change should happen over time and then—"

"Then?"

"The real transformation will happen when it will be noticed the most." Rena leaned in and curved her lips into a wickedly satisfied smile. "Cinderella will turn into a plain Jane, at the ball…my wedding!"

Four

Dressed in a Brooks Brothers suit and ready to stand up for Tony as best man, Joe glanced around the grounds of the Carlino estate. The backyard had been transformed into an elegant wedding venue, the changes subtle and well-designed thanks to Ali Pendrake.

Joe had spent the past weeks working on the wedding details with her, but she hadn't really needed his input. Ali's organizational skills and her instincts were right on. She'd ordered the cake, taken care of table seating arrangements, hired a five-piece band and a florist and arranged for her neighbor, Royce, to head up the catering.

Joe hadn't said much about her choice of chef, but he hadn't loved the idea.

She'd gotten here early this morning, dressed in jeans and an old sweatshirt, making sure everything would go according to plan. Joe couldn't commend her highly enough, but he also felt a personal sense of pride in her accomplishments. He hated to admit it, but Ali would make an expert wedding planner. Thank goodness, she seemed content working at Carlino Wines with him. He'd never be able to replace her.

"The place looks great," Tony said with a smile, coming to stand beside him on the patio. Guests milled around the grounds, conversing.

"You should tell Ali that. She did it all."

"I will. She's in with Rena now, getting dressed. They've become friends."

"Ali has no trouble making friends." Satisfaction hummed through him. Inexplicably, that his sister-in-law liked Ali made Joe feel good.

"Rena and I owe you both a big thank-you."

Joe nodded. "It wasn't as hard as I thought it'd be."

"Hell, I wouldn't think so. I hear you spent your weekends with Ali."

Joe shot his brother a warning glance. "It's not like that."

Tony shook his head. "I know, and I can't figure that out."

"Sometimes, neither can I." Joe muttered aloud what he'd kept his mind from thinking.

The band started playing, and guests began to take their seats. Tony straightened his tie and took a deep breath. "It's time to do this. I'd better get Rena."

Joe embraced his brother. "I'll see you up there," he said. "I'm happy for you, Tony."

Ali's plan was for both Tony and Rena to walk down the white aisle runner together. They'd had a hard road getting to this place, and their trip down the aisle together would be more meaningful and show unity.

Joe had the urge to grab Ali from the dressing room and have her stand beside him. He wanted her next to him.

They'd been together in this from the beginning, but he held back. Logically, his place was beside his brothers and not with his personal assistant. And damn it, if Ali had a way of making him think illogically.

Joe took his place next to Nick to the left of the flowery archway. The setting sun reflected off the pool waters, and he squinted as he waited for the wedding couple. The band stopped playing, and the entire group of guests hushed their voices. Then a harpist began playing a melodic tune.

Joe searched the dozens of guests for Ali. When he spotted her standing by the last row of chairs, their eyes locked.

His heart pounded.

His breath caught in his throat.

Dressed in a soft jade-colored satin dress, covered with a jacket of the same material, her hair spun up in a demure twist and her face nearly free of makeup, Joe almost hadn't recognized her. Her appearance stunned him. Flashy Ali, usually with all the bangles, beads, boots and exotic hair, looked soft and elegant tonight.

"That's a new look," Nick whispered. "Ali sure can keep a man on his toes."

Irritated by the truth of that comment, he ignored his brother and focused on Ali. She'd been on his mind too much lately. True, they'd spent a good deal of time together these past three weeks planning the wedding. Joe hadn't faltered, keeping his relationship perfectly professional the entire time. Whenever his mind would wander, he reminded himself that she was his employee and a woman who was off-limits. He denied feeling anything but pride for Ali and her accomplishments here today.

Joe turned his attention to his brother, who had reached the arbor of flowers along with Rena. Without the benefit of clergy, they renewed their wedding vows to each other with deep emotion and honesty. At times, they laughed; at times, tears stung their eyes. When it was all said and done, Tony took his pregnant wife by the hand and turned to their guests, receiving a round of applause.

Rena's face beamed with joy, and Tony looked happier than Joe had ever seen him. A bit of envy crept into his heart. At one time, Joe thought he could be that happy. But he'd learned a hard lesson. No woman would ever make a fool of him ever again.

After shaking his brother's hand and hugging Rena, Joe turned to face Ali, who had walked up and also congratulated the couple.

"You did it, Ali," he said.

"*We* did it, Joe," she said softly.

"You did most of the work. The place looks great. I can't give you high enough praise."

Ali put her head down, then glanced out toward the vineyards. "Thank you."

Joe was at a loss for words. Usually Ali did most of the talking. Today she appeared unusually melancholy. "Can I get you a drink?"

"That would be nice."

"I'll be right back."

Joe flagged down a waiter holding a tray of bubbly champagne and returned to Ali with two flutes. "Here you go." He handed her one and then made a toast. "To you, Ali, for all your hard work. The wedding was perfect."

Ali touched his glass and then sipped champagne.

Joe stared into her eyes, wondering what was up.

Ali smiled softly at him, and for some odd reason, dread entered his heart.

Ali's neighbor, Royce, came out of the kitchen and approached them. "Ali, can I speak with you for a minute? I need your opinion about something."

"Sure," she said to Royce. "Excuse me, Joe."

The chef put his hand to Ali's back and escorted her into the kitchen. With a clenched jaw, Joe watched Ali walk away from him. He polished off his champagne in one huge gulp and searched for something stronger.

He headed for the bar inside the house and poured himself two fingers of Scotch. It went down smooth and easy, and Joe sighed, relaxing his tense body.

Laughter from the kitchen had him walking that way. He stopped just outside the door, recognizing Royce's amusement and Ali's quiet chuckling. He heard Ali reassuring Royce about the main dish he planned to serve, complimenting his choice, and then they seemed to share another private joke.

Jealousy burned in his gut.

He clenched his teeth again and headed outside, his blood boiling.

Ali sat next to Joe at the Carlino table during dinner. She met Rena's good friends, Solena and Raymond, who worked at Purple Fields, and several of the Carlino cousins as they dined on Royce's amazing dinner. She'd had her doubts about hiring him since she sensed Joe didn't like him, but Royce's entrées were a big hit, and she felt justified in her choice.

She was sure she was only asked to join the head table because of the work she'd done on the wedding, yet everyone she'd met had been cordial to her. She'd bitten her tongue a dozen times dying to dive in and get to know her dining partners better, but she'd taken Rena's advice to stay under the radar instead of flashing her friendliness like a neon sign.

She'd spent the past three weekends with Joe, creating a wedding and reception that Tony and Rena would cherish in their memories. All that time, Joe had been eager to help, but he hadn't shown one iota of interest in her personally, even though she'd become more reserved, put her hair into sedate styles she'd never have dreamed up before and dressed herself like a churchgoing schoolteacher.

Her ego had taken a deep plunge.

This was her last-ditch effort to get Joe to notice her as more than his employee. If the makeover in reverse was her ticket to gain Joe's attention, then she'd give it her best shot. Unfortunately, patience was a virtue she hadn't been born with. She'd wanted this to happen the second she'd slipped her feet into her first pair of lackluster pumps.

"In case I haven't said it yet, you look very beautiful tonight," Nick said from across the round table. Rena had done the seating cards and had deliberately put Joe next to her and Nick as far away as possible. "Joe, don't you think so?"

Joe shot Nick a hard look and then turned to Ali. Needlessly, he pushed his glasses up his nose. They were already as far as they could go. "Yes, Ali, you look very pretty tonight."

Nick grinned, and Ali didn't know which Carlino brother she should clobber first.

"Thank you both."

Ali looked at Rena, who gave her a nod of approval. Rena had been a saint, helping her pick out a new conservative wardrobe and giving her tips on how to subdue her outgoing personality. Rena warned it might take some time for this plan to work, but Ali wondered how long she could endure loving Joe and not having that love returned.

After dinner, the band started up again, and people began to approach the large redwood decking overlooking the vineyards, which served as the dance floor.

Ali rose from the dinner table to listen to the music,

and immediately, a friend of the family approached her. "Would you care to dance?"

Ali didn't have time to respond. Joe appeared beside her and clasped her hand in his. "I think she promised me the first dance, Allen."

Ali's heart pumped overtime. Joe squeezed her hand tight, and she nearly stumbled when he brought her onto the dance floor. "I don't do fast," he warned.

How well she knew. But she was sure he meant fast *dances.*

"But I think I can manage not to break your toes with this song." He pulled her up against him, and she thought she'd died and gone to heaven. Hugo cologne and dancing practically cheek to cheek with Joe was a sexy mix. Consumed with being in his arms, she couldn't name the artist or the song they danced to, barely hearing the music at all as Joe swirled her slowly around the dance floor.

"You're a good dancer, Joe."

"Am I?" he asked, his voice a low rasp in her ear.

Tingles broke out all over her body, and she relished each amazing second of the dance.

Joe tightened his hold on her. "How can I thank you for tonight?" he whispered.

She had a few suggestions that didn't involve touring Napa. Lusty images filled her head. She could barely put together a coherent thought with him holding her so close. But she couldn't push her luck. She had to stick to the plan. "You didn't forget our bargain, did you?"

"No. I'm a man of my word."

"I know that about you."

Joe pulled away to gaze into her eyes. He blinked a few times and then shot her a killer smile. That smile, his sexy scent, the way he held her—Ali wanted to pull him into his bedroom and make love to him until the sun came up.

"I'm glad, Ali, but I just don't know how much you'll get out of me being your tour guide."

Nick and Royce both offered to show her the sights, but Ali was holding out for numero uno. She wanted to spend time with Joe and only Joe. Ali had pressed him to this bargain, and she couldn't let him off the hook now. Normally, she'd goad him into it—a promise is a promise—but the new Ali had to take a different turn. "It's all right if you'd rather not. I understand."

Joe's brows arched. "I wasn't weaseling out of it, Ali. I'll do my best to show you around."

Ali smiled, warmth overflowing. "That's all I ask."

Joe seemed satisfied with that and took her back into his arms until the dance ended. When they parted, Ali hated the separation. She could have stayed on the dance floor with Joe all night.

"Thanks for the dance," he said, escorting her back to their table.

"It was nice, Joe. Thank you."

Joe nodded, and when he pulled out her chair to sit down, Ali changed her mind about staying at the table. "I think I'll take a little walk."

"Would you like some company?"

She would love it! She hesitated one second then with a slight tilt of her head, she answered. "Okay."

They walked past the reception area lit with twinkle lights and lanterns, down an inlaid stone pathway that led to steep steps. Only moonlight guided their way now, the party music fading.

"They're tricky without much light." Joe took her hand and helped her down steps that seemed to go on forever. He'd touched her more today than in the past year since she'd met him. Ali held out some hope that progress was being made, small as it may be.

Once they reached the floor of the vineyard, which was still pretty high up on the hillside, he released her hand. Ali gazed out at the endless rows of vines that columned Carlino land. She sighed in awe. "Most people have swing sets in their backyards."

"We had those, too. We were privileged as kids, but believe it or not, we had a pretty normal childhood. My father was a taskmaster. We had chores to do and had to bring home good grades, just like anybody else. We got grounded. Well, I didn't so much, but Nick and Tony? They were always causing the old man conniptions."

Ali wished her childhood involved having a mother and father who loved her unconditionally. Someone who loved her enough to ground her or make sure she was doing her homework. She'd never had stability in her life. There was never much normalcy, either. Joe—living up here on a hill, with all his wealth and privileges—probably did have a more normal childhood than she had.

"He cared about the men you were to become."

Joe scrubbed his jaw. "I guess so. He was a hard man. My mother softened him, though. He loved her so much. He'd have died for her."

"They were lucky to have each other."

Ali turned from Joe to absorb what he'd just said. She pretended to look out at the vineyards, but she looked beyond them to her own life. That kind of love—that close family bond—was completely foreign to her. People looked at her and assumed she had everything she wanted. But that was far from the truth. Her childhood hadn't been a fairy tale. She wanted the kind of love that Joe's mother had—that unconditional commitment and devotion. Ali had been on her own in one way or another most of her life.

She could easily live a superficial life, the kind her mother lived, bouncing in and out of relationships, grasping for the brass ring that would make her happy momentarily, but never fully content. Ali had vowed to never be like her mother. She wanted something real. Money didn't matter to her. Oddly, she'd fallen for Joe, a man worth millions, but he could just as well have been broke and she still would've loved him. That was the difference between her and her mother.

"Ali, are you okay?" Joe came up behind her, his voice soft and tender. She felt his solid presence at her back. Maybe that's why she loved him. Joe was a rock of stability. "You're different tonight."

Tears entered her eyes, and she fought them. She couldn't break down in front of him. She didn't want his pity. She didn't want to tell him about her mother, her past and the love she'd never received as a child.

Taking a deep breath, she turned to him and gave a little shrug. "Weddings do that to me. I'm fine."

"You're quiet. I thought you loved a good party." Joe searched her eyes. He looked puzzled and sweetly concerned.

Oh, how she hated all this deception. She just wanted to blurt out that she loved him. She loved him, and her heart was breaking. But it was the last thing Joe would want to hear. She'd destroy their relationship. She had to follow through with "the plan."

"I'm enjoying myself."

Joe cast her a dubious look. "Have I done anything to upset you?"

She shook her head. "No."

To her surprise, Joe reached for both of her hands, clasping them tight. An unexpected jolt shot clear through her. She held her breath, her heart hammering.

Joe slanted his head, staring deep into her eyes and

leaned toward her. "Maybe I'm about to," he whispered into her mouth.

Then he pressed his lips to hers.

The kiss was gentle and giving, but that didn't stop fireworks from exploding in her head. She could hardly believe this. Joy entered her heart, and she wanted to wrap her arms around his neck and press her body against him.

Please let this moment never end.

Joe must have heard her silent plea. He slid his hands up her arms and gently squeezed, tugging her closer, his hips crinkling her satin gown as he deepened the kiss.

The rich taste of liquor made her head swim, and images of bedrooms and silken sheets flashed in her mind. Joe parted her lips and their tongues mated, then a deep groan of pleasure rumbled from his throat and Ali's joy doubled.

It was finally happening.

"Hey, Joe? You down there?" Nick called from above. "It's time to toast the bride and groom."

Ali gasped when she heard Nick's voice and backed away.

"I'll be right there," Joe called toward the stairs. She couldn't see Nick, which meant he couldn't have seen what Joe and Ali had been doing.

Joe turned to her. "Sorry. We'd better get back. You okay?" he asked, blinking behind his glasses.

She couldn't utter a word, so she bobbed her head up and down.

"I, uh, should explain," Joe began, his voice a rasp in the breeze. "You looked like you needed…comforting." Joe's brows furrowed as if he was as confused by his confession as she was.

"Comforting?" Ali questioned on a low breath.

"Yeah." Then Joe turned his attention toward the stairs. "C'mon." He took her hand, and they climbed up the steps, Ali following behind him. Before they reached the top of the stairs, he turned to her, his gaze fastened to her mouth. "When I said I was sorry, I didn't mean about kissing you. I meant sorry we were interrupted."

"I think I knew that," Ali replied, just catching her breath.

Joe's lips curled up slightly. "You're astute, Ali, but if I was out of line, you'd tell me, right?"

Heavens, he was so *in* line, it wasn't even funny. "Yes, I'd be sure to tell you."

Joe looked at her mouth one last time with regret in his eyes, and Ali wanted to skip right over the moon.

After the toasts were made by Joe and Nick, everyone sipped champagne and wished the newlyweds the best. Rena sidled up next to Ali by the dance floor. "How's it going, my friend?"

Ali beamed her a smile. "I'm no longer in the potted plant category."

Rena's brows rose, and she looked on with interest. "Really?"

"Joe kissed me down in the vineyards," she gushed out. She'd wanted to scream it from the rooftops that Joe Carlino finally showed some interest in her. "It was *the best.*"

"What did he say?"

"Not much. He was worried about me. I think this change really threw him off. He's looking a little bit puzzled."

"He noticed you. That's all that matters."

Ali drew in a deep breath and sighed. "Oh, I know, but I'm not patient enough to wait. I want more."

Rena's chuckle turned a few heads in her direction.

"Calm down, Ali. You're doing fine. And you look stunning in that dress."

"Who knew that I could wear something so…not me and pull it off?"

"I did."

"Well, I'm not counting my chickens yet."

"It takes time, Ali. If it's meant to be, it'll happen." she said. "And look who's coming straight toward us, with you in his sights."

Ali glanced across the decking and spotted Joe, heading her way. Every time she looked at him dressed in that striking black suit, his dark hair groomed just so, his handsome face marred by just a hint of a beard and wearing those glasses that made him look sexier than a man had a right to look, her heart rate sped up like crazy.

Rena leaned over to whisper. "Remember, weddings have a way of bringing out the best in people."

Ali swallowed hard.

Joe focused his attention on her as he approached. "Is it time to cut the cake?"

Joe was always spot on when it came to schedules. "Yes, I think it's time." She turned to Rena. "Ready?"

"I'm ready. I'll find Tony and meet you over by the cake table."

Both watched as Rena walked away. "I think everyone had a great time tonight," Joe said.

"I know I did."

Joe gazed into her eyes. "I'm feeling a little bit guilty," he began, and Ali prayed he didn't regret their kiss from a few minutes ago. She waited for him to explain. "A few people asked me if you were a party planner. You could have a very lucrative business here, if you wanted it."

"So why are you guilty?"

"Because I told them you're not interested in outside work. You did this as a favor to the family."

"That's not a lie."

"Well no, not technically. But I shouldn't have answered for you. The fact is, I don't want to lose you," then Joe hesitated before adding, "as my personal assistant."

Ali smiled inwardly. Joe was slowly coming around. "You won't."

Joe stared at her, unblinking then glanced at her lips. She returned his stare, wishing he'd kiss her again. But she knew that he wouldn't in full view of the guests at the reception. Too many people knew Ali worked for Joe, and his reputation was at stake, along with hers.

The irony struck her anew. Ali never wanted an office romance. She'd shied away from them all of her adult life, wanting to be treated as an equal in business and respected for her intellect. And as soon as she found a man who'd done that, she'd fallen hard for him.

"I'm in the mood for something sweet," Joe said, still glancing at her mouth.

"Hmm?" She cast him a curious look. It wasn't like Joe to make innuendo. Could he have been teasing?

He gestured with a slight nod toward the fondant cake decorated with white roses and greenery. "Cake. Let's go and see how good your pastry chef is."

He's not *her* pastry chef. She'd simply hired him, but Ali stifled her comment. "I'd like that. Royce recommended him highly."

Joe's lips twisted but he didn't reply.

And ten minutes later, Ali sat at their table in sugar heaven. The mango-filled white cake was too delicious for words. "Mmm."

"It's pretty damn good." Joe had his piece of cake polished off in seconds.

Ali scooped up the last bit of frosting with her fork, relishing every bite, aware that Joe watched her every move. When the owner of a neighboring winery stopped by the table asking to speak to Joe for a second, he agreed and rose from his seat, bending to whisper in her ear. "Excuse me, I'll be right back."

Goose bumps erupted on her arms, and Ali's body sizzled. She cast him a quick acknowledgment and watched him leave. This was new for her. She'd never received so much attention from Joe, and she wanted it to continue. The handsome prince had kissed her and stolen her heart. But she feared her reverse Cinderella night was quickly coming to an end. Now what?

The final dance of the evening was announced. Everyone stopped their conversations and mingled around the dance floor. The band played an old classic tune "I Want to Walk You Home," and Rena, dressed in an ivory-colored satin maternity dress, swirled around on Tony's arm, glowing with joy.

Their happiness was contagious, and as Ali glanced around, she found smiles on all the guests' faces. Out of the blue, Royce appeared next to her.

"Give me a rain check on a dance," he said. "I couldn't get away long enough to show you my dance skills."

He'd changed from his chef's uniform into dark slacks and a black shirt. She couldn't deny her neighbor his good looks. She'd noticed more than one female's head turn in his direction during the night.

"That's okay, Royce. You showed me your culinary skills."

"Well?"

"Absolutely perfect. Every dish was delicious."

Royce closed his eyes, savoring the compliment. "Thank

you, Ali. You recommended me for this event, and I didn't want to let you down."

"You didn't," she said. Then she tilted her head. "In fact, you exceeded my expectations."

"The same can be said about you. You put this party together in record time, and it looked as if you'd worked on it for months instead of weeks."

They shared a moment of mutual admiration.

"Let me finish up in the kitchen, and I'll drive you home," Royce said.

"I'm taking Ali home."

Ali turned to find Joe beside her, his jaw tight as he faced Royce. Where had he come from? Ali hadn't seen him since he'd taken off to speak with that elderly winemaker.

"It's not a problem," Royce said. "We live in the same building."

Joe removed his glasses slowly, squaring off with Royce. Neither one of the men looked like they'd back down. Ali felt like a pawn in some macho game. "Actually, I have my own car. But thank you both for the offer."

There, she'd settled it.

Joe hesitated, eyeing Royce, then slipped his glasses back on. "The food was exceptional tonight."

Royce seemed surprised at the compliment. His rigid stance relaxed some. "Thank you."

That's what she loved about Joe. He was fair-minded. "Ali recommended you, and I trust her judgment."

"I'm happy to have the honor." Royce glanced at Ali. "I've got to see to the cleanup in the kitchen. Catch you later, Ali."

"See you, Royce."

Ali turned to face Joe, his expression noncommittal. "I'll be leaving shortly, unless there's anything else you need me to do?"

"No, you've outdone yourself with this party. Tony and Rena are thrilled with how it all turned out. I am, too."

"It was a pleasure," she said. "Well, then I'd better say good-night to them." She turned to leave.

"Wait," Joe said firmly. "It's a difficult drive down the hill at night. You don't know the roads. I'll follow you."

"But you don't have—"

"No arguments, Ali. I'm following you home."

Five

Joe followed behind Ali's car until she parked in her garage. He watched her get out. He debated for a half second whether to get out of the car and walk her to the door, a little war waging in his head.

The kiss they shared earlier was still on his mind. He'd been foolish to do it, yet he hadn't been able to stop himself. Ali had looked vulnerable and a little sad, something he'd not recognized in her before. The change in her made him want to comfort and console her. He'd meant to plant a little peck on her lips, but the minute he'd taken her into his arms, something snapped inside him. He wanted to hold her and go on holding her. To kiss her and go on kissing her.

He wanted to do more.

Warning bells rang out in his head. His mind screamed that she was off-limits. He wasn't ready for any relationship, much less one with his employee. How many times had he reminded himself of that?

Joe stepped out of his car and leaned against it. "Thank you for following me home, Joe. It wasn't necessary, but I do appreciate it."

"Just wanted to make sure you got home safely, Ali."

She faced him and leaned over to give him a little kiss on his cheek. "That's sweet."

Sweet? Joe's hackles went up. He spread his legs and braced Ali's waist with his hands, pulling her closer. Her exotic scent scurried up his nose and went straight to his brain. "Can you forget that I'm your boss for one night?"

His gaze dropped down to the ripe fullness of her mouth.

Ali blinked. Then a beautiful smile emerged. "I think so. Why?"

Joe answered her by wrapping a hand around her neck and bringing her mouth to his. "To show you I'm not that sweet," he whispered before he crushed his mouth to hers.

A tiny whimper of pleasure arose from Ali's throat, her lips inviting and lush. Joe deepened the kiss and brought Ali even closer, meshing their hips together.

Pressure built in his groin, his breathing sped up and the urge to take Ali inside her apartment and finish this overwhelmed him. He mated their tongues, all the while stroking his knuckles along her smooth cheekbones and then capturing her face in his outspread hand.

"Still think I'm sweet?" he asked, nipping at her lower lip.

"Not at the moment," she answered without hesitation.

"Am I out of line?" he whispered.

She sighed into his mouth. "Very."

But she wasn't complaining, and that's all the fuel Joe

needed to continue. His mind went on autopilot, and he kissed her again and again, each time bringing her closer, crushing her beautiful breasts to his chest, his arousal hard to restrain.

He stroked her lower back, gliding his hands up and down, damning the satin material and wishing he could put his palms to her creamy skin.

Ali pulled away slightly, her breathing labored, a soft sheen on her face. She searched his eyes and shook her head. "I don't do one-night stands, Joe."

Joe loosened his hold on her. It was hard to let her go. Already, he missed the sweetness of her mouth on his and her erotic scent filling his head. He pursed his lips and nodded. He'd let his lust get in the way of what he knew to be right. "When I asked if you could forget that I was your boss for one night, that's really not what I had in mind. I, uh, things got a little carried away."

"They seem to, whenever you kiss me," Ali stated quietly.

Joe knew better than to mess with Ali's emotions. Nothing could come of their relationship. He was her boss, and she was his most trusted employee. "Listen, uh, I, don't believe in workplace relationships. I did that once, and let's just say that it was painful and destructive."

Ali listened patiently, her gaze intent on him. She looked so lovely tonight, and any other man would have found it easy to seduce her into bed. Joe still wanted to. He wanted to make love to Ali tonight.

But it wasn't fair to her, and he'd vowed that he'd never put himself in that situation again.

He reached into his pocket and pulled out a jewelry box made of gold velvet. "This is what I'd meant." He handed Ali the box, laying it on her palm. "It's a thank-you for all you've done to help me."

Ali gazed at the box she held. "I don't understand."

"A pay bonus didn't seem quite right in thanking you for what you've done tonight. You helped my family, and that called for something more personal. I can't tell you how much I appreciate, well...you. Open it."

With trembling hands, Ali opened the box. The look on her face made it all worthwhile. "It's beautiful."

"I picked it out, but I wasn't sure you'd like it."

Joe had gone to the best jeweler in the county to find just the right gold and diamond bracelet. He was used to seeing Ali wearing bangles and jewelry that made a big statement. But that wasn't what he'd wanted for her. When he'd spotted this bracelet, he knew it was right for her. It wasn't gaudy—the small, but perfect diamonds were set within the gold framework of the delicate piece.

"I love it," she said softly. Then her eyes filled with moisture. "This is a thank-you?"

He nodded. "For everything, Ali. But mostly for making my brother's wedding so memorable. Do you want to try it on?"

She nodded and Joe lifted the bracelet from the box and took her wrist in his hand. He secured the clasp, his head bumping hers as they looked on. Her subtle exotic scent dazzled him. Their heads came up at the same time, and they stared into each other's eyes.

Joe's heart thumped, a spark of something more than lust making its way in. He kept thinking of the torturous night ahead while he slept alone in his bed, yet knowing he'd made the right decision.

I don't do one-night stands.

And that's all Joe could offer her. He released her hand.

"It fits perfectly." Ali's voice lowered until it was barely audible. "You *are* sweet."

Joe cringed inwardly.

Ali smiled, and he wasn't sure what to make of it. She blinked and took a deep breath that was almost a sigh of disappointment. "Well, I'd better get inside. I'll probably fall asleep the minute my head hits the pillow."

Joe wished he'd be that lucky. He already knew what his night would be like. "Good night, Ali."

"Good night, Joe."

He waited for her to get inside and close her garage door before he got into his car and drove away.

Ali leaned against the garage door of her condo, listening as Joe drove off. She fingered the bracelet on her wrist, with love bursting from her heart. She'd never been given such a beautiful, thoughtful gift and yet, she'd let Joe leave tonight, making it clear that she wasn't a woman who slept with men unless there was a commitment.

It was the vow she'd made to herself after watching her mother's social-climbing ways. If Joe wasn't ready to give her more, then Ali would have to wait.

But the waiting was killing her! She could be in bed with Joe, making love with him at this very moment if she hadn't stopped him, yet she'd had to express her feelings. He hadn't offered her more than a night of passion, and Ali wouldn't settle for that. She wanted Joe—but not just for one night. She wanted his love and respect, too.

She learned a hard lesson allowing a man to call all the shots. Ali knew better now. Judging by the press of Joe's arousal while kissing her, Joe would have definitely made her night memorable. Sadness filled her heart for a moment, but then she remembered what Rena said.

Be patient.

She realized Rena was right. After all, she'd made progress, and turning Joe away tonight might not have been a bad thing. All things considered, the night had been magical, and Joe had certainly noticed her.

Ali took a quick hot shower and dressed for bed. She climbed in, tucking herself in cozily, and laid her head back, relishing the softness of her pillow. When the phone rang, she groaned and let it ring again, pretending she hadn't heard it. On the fifth insistent ring, she grabbed for it grudgingly, glancing at the clock. It was after midnight, and she couldn't imagine who'd be calling this late. "Hello."

"Ali, it's me."

Those three words instilled fear in her heart when she recognized the voice. She bolted up from bed. "Mom, what's wrong?" Her mother lived on the East Coast, and it was three in the morning there. Concern rippled through her. Guiltily she realized she hadn't talked to her mother in over a month. "Are you okay?"

"No, I'm not okay. I'm terrible." Her mother sobbed into the phone, alarming Ali all the more. Visions of her contracting a rare disease or having a car accident flashed through Ali's mind.

"What is it?"

"It's Harold. He's being impossible. I don't think I can live with him anymore."

Ali's rigid shoulders slumped.

Not this again.

She recognized her mother's tone and the sobs that were more complaint than anguish. What was it this time? Was his work interfering with their playtime? Or was Harold smoking too much? Maybe he liked his dog more than her. Ali had heard it all before. Her mother's need for attention and adoration was monumental, and whenever she didn't get it from one husband, she'd move on.

At forty-nine, her mother was still a beauty, and she had no trouble attracting men. Her problem was keeping them.

She expected perfection from her mate, when she was far from it herself. She wanted to be placed on a pedestal and admired by her man. It had become increasingly clear to Ali that the main trouble with her mother's relationships with men was that *life* got in her way.

There were times when her mother couldn't be the main focus in her husband's life. Times when their work took precedence and times when outside influences that couldn't be helped, interfered. Ali had always believed that the men Justine had married truly loved her, but they couldn't keep up with Justine's need for attention.

"Mom, what's wrong with Harold?" Ali had actually *liked* Harold Holcomb. He was a man of honor and integrity and had always treated her mother well in their three years of marriage.

"He's being so…so, stubborn."

"Mom, please stop crying."

"Okay," she said immediately, catching a sob. "I know you hate when I cry."

"I do. You know I've always liked Harold. I think you should calm down and think about what's important in life. *Really* important."

"I know you think I'm flighty, but this time I'm really worried. We're always fighting and… Ali, *I really love Harold.*"

Her mother seemed a little stunned by her own revelation. Maybe she'd finally figured out what love was all about. "He loves you, too, Mom."

"I know."

"Then whatever it is, you two can work it out."

"I know, I know. You've already said you won't come to any more weddings so I'd better make this one stick."

"Mom," Ali said, sighing into the phone, "can we discuss this in the morning? I'm really tired."

"It's only midnight there, sweetie."

"That's late for us working girls."

"But surely you're not working tomorrow—on Sunday?"

"No, I'm not." Yes, she actually was. She'd brought home a stack of work to look over. She'd been so busy with the wedding reception this week that she'd put a few projects on hold, knowing she'd get to them on Sunday.

Not that her mother had asked her how she liked her new job or her new home. When Ali had moved here from the East Coast, her mother had called her once to make sure she was settled and safe. Once she was assured of that, she hadn't called again, leaving it up to Ali to make the calls from then on.

Her mother really did love her, but she showed it in odd ways sometimes. This call tonight was a perfect example of her love. Justine confided in Ali when she wouldn't confide in anyone else. Ali had always shared that bond with her mom. She'd listen to her and give advice and encouragement, and her mother always made it clear that Ali was the only one she trusted to vent her frustrations.

Maybe Ali had been far too understanding with her mom over the years. Justine needed a hefty dose of reality. "I had a big day today, Mom. I helped my boss plan a wedding reception all week, and tonight was the big event. I just got in a few minutes ago, and I'm really pooped."

"Your boss? You mean, Joe Carlino?"

"Yes, I mean, Joe."

"How was the affair?"

"Spectacular, even if I do say so myself."

"If you had anything to do with it, I'm sure it was stylish and fun."

"Thanks, Mom." Justine was loyal and thought Ali could

conquer the world. Another example of how she showed her love.

Ali wondered what her mother would think of the "new-and-improved" Ali Pendrake, the one with the conservative clothes and reserved demeanor. The one who'd sink to fraudulent behavior to ensnare the man of her dreams.

Justine never had to resort to such measures. She'd simply flirt and tease a man to garner his interest, but Ali was sure her mother had never come up against anyone like Joe before. A man like Joe wouldn't interest her enough to make overtures.

Yet, Joe held Ali's heart in the palm of his hand.

"Okay, sweetie," her mother said. "I'll call you in the morning." She sniffled. "It was good to hear your voice. I miss you, Ali."

Ali closed her eyes and savored the sentiment. "I miss you, too, Mom."

She really did.

"Good night. Sleep tight. You're my beautiful princess."

Ali smiled into the phone. "I know. Good night, Mom."

On Monday morning, Joe walked into the Carlino Wines office, amazed at how this century-old building had survived to modern times. The building on Main Street was well known as one of the "ghost wineries" of the past that had been nearly crippled by age and ruin. The exterior built of mortar and stone, refurbished to its original vintage architecture, spoke of winemaking in its earliest form in the Napa region.

While the exterior held the ambience of old times, the interior had been transformed into offices that represented the most modern and up-to-date technology and equipment in the country. For all his old ways, Joe's father, Santo Carlino, had also been a forward thinker.

Joe headed past the reception area and aimed his way toward his office, stopping short as he approached Ali's outer office. He blinked his eyes then drew his brows together.

Ali sat at her desk, her gaze focused on her computer screen. Her auburn hair was drawn severely back and clasped at the nape of her neck with a band, and her face, free of makeup was adorned with plain, wire-rimmed eyeglasses. He approached with caution. "Ali?"

"Hi, Joe," she said, barely casting him a glance. "Just catching up on work."

He swallowed. "I didn't know you wore glasses."

Ali stopped what she was doing to grant him a little smile. "My contacts were bothering me under the fluorescent lights. I think I need to see my eye doctor." She shrugged. "It's just easier to wear glasses at work." She tilted her head to one side. "Do you mind?"

"Mind?" Joe stepped back a half step. "No, of course not." He pushed his own glasses farther up his nose. "I just didn't realize you wore them."

Ali stood up and came around the desk. "I came in early to finish up those reports you'd asked for." She handed them to him, and Joe noticed the diamond bracelet around her wrist.

His heart gladdened at the sight.

She wore no other jewelry but a pair of tiny heart-shaped gold earrings.

Joe took the files from her. The brush of her hand against his created an immediate spark. They stared at each other, their eyes behind their eyeglasses, locking. Then he scanned her body, taking in her soft pink knit sweater and straight-leg, gray slacks. Something was way off, and it had little to do with the clothes she wore. Joe couldn't put a finger on it until his eyes ventured farther down her body to her feet.

She wore flats. Aside from the glasses and clothes being different, Joe realized he towered over her by three *extra* inches. "You're shorter today." He hadn't meant to blurt that out.

Ali stifled a giggle. "That's what happens when I don't wear high heels."

Joe smiled, reminded of the night he'd fixed her computer, after she'd come out of the shower. She'd been barefoot, but he hadn't noticed how he'd towered over her. He'd had other things to focus on then. In the workplace, though, it caught him off guard. "I guess so."

"Anything else?" she asked.

"No, not at all." Joe tapped the file against his other hand. "Thanks for this. There was no rush on it."

Ali sat behind her desk. "It wasn't a problem. I came in early."

Joe continued to stare. He couldn't help from peering at her mouth and remembering how her lips felt pressed up to his. The kisses they shared the other night couldn't be repeated, yet they'd stayed with him all weekend long. If he were honest with himself, he'd have to say the memory had haunted him.

He remembered holding her and pulling her against him, having her body pressed to his, his desire evident and obvious to both of them. He shoved that memory aside and instead recalled the joy he'd witnessed on her face when he'd given her the bracelet.

Putting it on her.

Seeing her green eyes sparkle as bright as those diamonds.

Feeling contentment that he'd made her happy.

"Joe," Ali was saying, holding the phone to her ear. "You have a call, line two."

"Oh," he said, coming out of his reverie. "Thanks, I'll get it in my office."

"Mr. Carlino will be right with you," Ali said into the phone, and Joe strode to his office and closed the door.

The rest of the week had been pretty much the same. Joe found himself immersed in Ali. He stole glances at her whenever the mood struck, watched her talk on the phone or interact with other employees. She'd play with a rebellious lock of her upswept hair as she studied something on her computer screen, and Joe's methodical mind would wander to the land of Ali Pendrake.

"This is crazy," he muttered to himself on Friday afternoon. He'd been avoiding spending more time with her than necessary, but he owed her. And Joe was a man of his word.

He shot up from his chair and walked over to her desk. She peered up at him over her glasses, and Joe thought she looked adorably sexy.

Don't go there, Carlino.

Those thoughts were exactly why he'd procrastinated all week long.

"Do you need something, Joe?"

"Ali, this is really short notice."

"What is?" She looked puzzled and glanced at her watch. "If you need those invoices sooner, I'm on top of it. They're almost done."

"No, it's not about invoices." Joe scratched his head. "Do you have plans tomorrow?"

"Saturday? Well, nothing that can't be changed. I can come in if it's urgent."

Joe shook his head and stared at the diamond bracelet

he'd given her. She'd worn it every day this week. "This isn't about work."

She stopped what she was doing and took off her glasses. Her eyes were the prettiest shade of light jade. Joe leaned over her desk, bracing his hands on the edge. "I thought you might like to see some of the sights in Napa."

Realization dawned, and Ali pursed her lips, drawing his attention there. Her mouth looked glossy and soft pink, kissable. He forced his attention back up to her eyes.

Ali drew in a breath, then sighed. "Joe, I know you don't want to do this."

The disappointment registering on her face made him feel like a heel. He shouldn't have waited until the last minute. From the look in her eyes, he could tell she'd let him off the hook. Yet, suddenly, that's the last thing Joe wanted. "I do, Ali."

"Because you owe me?" she asked softly.

"Because we made a deal, and I want to show you—"

"Show me?"

"Around. I'd like to show you around wine country. I've been checking out some places during the week that I thought you'd like to see." The fib flowed easily through his lips.

"Really?"

Joe nodded. "Just tell me what time you can be ready."

"I just need to make a phone call to cancel a lesson."

"A lesson?"

She shook her head. "With Royce. He was going to teach me how to cook a—" Ali stopped in mid-sentence and made a slight gesture with her hand "—it's not important. He can show me another time."

Royce again? Joe was glad he'd foiled her plans with

Royce. He felt no compunction whatsoever, and a sly smile curved his lips. "How strong are your legs?"

Ali snapped her eyes to him. "My legs? Pretty strong, I guess. Why?"

She worked out. Joe remembered the night she'd opened the door to him in her workout clothes, her body gleaming with moisture. He'd also seen her going into the on-site gym during her lunch hour. "We're going on a bike trip. It'll take the whole day and into the evening. Are you up for it?"

Ali's expression brightened, and for a second, he thought she'd jump out of her chair. Then she took a deep breath and sent him a sweet smile. "Yes. I'm up for it."

"I'll pick you up at nine."

"Do I need to bring anything in particular?"

Joe shook his head. "I've got it covered."

Joe walked back to his office and sat behind his desk and waited until Ali left her desk. Then he called his friend from high school who ran the Napa Wine and Dine Bike Tour Company. "Hey, Benny. I'm calling in a favor. I need to arrange a private bike tour ASAP. Can I count on you?"

After his phone call with Benny, Joe leaned back, arms behind his head, and rocked in his leather seat, thinking about Ali and looking forward to spending the entire day with her.

An unexpected peace washed over him.

Joe bolted upright in his seat, coming to grips with what he was feeling for her.

Lust, Carlino, he told himself.

That's all it was.

He could deal with it.

He refused to admit it was anything more.

Six

Ali spent Friday night floating on air. She'd had a dickens of a time restraining herself when Joe had approached her at the office about the bike tour. She'd wanted to jump for joy, but instead she'd kept a reasonable sense of decorum. She sensed that when Joe gave her the diamond bracelet it was his way of getting out of their deal, yet he'd surprised her with the offer.

Excited, Ali picked up the phone and dialed Rena's number. She had to share the news with someone. When Rena picked up, Ali greeted her in a rushed voice. "It's Ali. Guess what? I'm going out with Joe tomorrow!"

"Oh, Ali. That's wonderful. So is our little plan working?"

Ali's joy ebbed a little, reminded of the deception that she'd engaged in with Joe. If there was any other way to get Joe's attention she would have tried it, but she couldn't look this gift horse in the mouth. "Apparently so. I'm so happy now that I could throw a party."

"You already did, for me. And it was perfect, Ali. So tell me all about this date."

Ali told her about the bike tour and then relayed the events of the past week and remarked that Rena had been right. Joe seemed to notice the more demure, subdued Ali more. At least, they'd been interacting on a personal level now.

Ali would do anything within her power to have her love returned by Joe, yet as she spoke with Rena, a thought wiggled into her subconscious that she wanted Joe to love her for herself—the woman she truly was.

Rena's bright voice broke into her thoughts. "I can't wait to see you in glasses, Ali. Nice touch."

"You'd hardly recognize me, Rena."

"You're beautiful with or without glasses, Ali. With or without flashy clothes. Joe will come to see this. Right now, you're giving him a very loud wake-up call."

Ali immediately felt better. Rena was right again. She'd needed to change things up a little to get Joe to look at her as more than his devoted assistant. Who'd have thunk she'd needed a reverse makeover to achieve her goals.

Yet, Joe wasn't like most men. And that's what she loved about him.

"I guess you're right, Rena. I hadn't really thought about it that way. I'm glad I called you. I was about to burst outta my seams."

Rena chuckled. "Hey, you're giving an old pregnant lady a thrill."

"Glad to help. Now, if only I could get some sleep tonight."

"Look who's talking about not sleeping. What if you had

twenty pounds of extra baby weight around your middle and no way to get comfortable."

"I wish," Ali said with longing.

Rena's tone sobered a minute. "You'll get there, Ali."

"Will I?"

"Remember what I said about being patient."

"I'm trying. But with every beat of my heart I want to jump Joe's bones and tell him how I feel."

Rena laughed. "Your time will come. Have faith."

"I do."

After Ali finished her conversation with Rena, she felt much better. She poured herself a glass of milk and grabbed an organic oatmeal cookie Royce had brought over the other day.

She sat down on her sofa, propped her feet up and clicked on the television remote. She found her favorite cooking show, munched on the cookie and sipped milk, settling in for a relaxing evening.

Not five minutes into *The Rachel Ray Show,* breaking news flashed on the screen. Images of a yacht off the Florida waters appeared, and the newscaster's somber tone alerted Ali immediately—she recognized the yacht. She leaned forward and turned up the volume on the television.

"While Senator Rodney Holcomb and his family vacationed off the coast of Florida on his yacht, Harold Holcomb, the senator's younger brother, had what is alleged to be a heart attack. The senator acted quickly administering CPR, but it is unknown whether his attempts helped to save his brother's life. Harold Holcomb was airlifted to West Palm Beach Memorial Hospital, along with his wife. The senator will be making a statement in the morning...."

Ali bounded up from the sofa and reached for her phone, dialing her mother's number. Thoughts of their last conversation ran through her head.

We're fighting all the time.

He's so strong-willed. He never gives in.

Her mother married a powerful man, a man who was accustomed to making all the decisions. Justine wouldn't let him get away with bulldozing her. She needed to have a say-so in their lives. Originally, according to her mother, it was what Harold liked best about her. She'd always challenged him.

And what had Ali told her mother to do?

Take a vacation. Get away from their routine and daily life. Take a cruise and talk things out.

Apparently, that's what they'd been doing, trying to work out their differences, perhaps.

Her mother's cell phone rang and rang. Ali's nerves went raw. After the sixth ring, finally someone picked up. "Mom, Mom, is that you? Are you okay?"

"This is Judy Holcomb. Is this Ali?"

It was the senator's wife. "Yes, it's me, Judy. Where's my mother?" Ali couldn't keep the panic out of her voice.

"We're in West Palm Beach Memorial Hospital. Your mom's in with Harry. She's pretty shaken up."

"And what about Harold? The news report said he had a heart attack."

"Yes, they've confirmed it now. They are running tests."

"I'm so sorry. Mom must be beside herself."

"Well, yes. I won't lie to you. She's quite upset. It was a shock to all of us. We were having such a nice time after dinner. Harold and your mother were walking on deck, and she came running for help, crying that Harry had collapsed. We assumed it was a heart attack, and Rodney gave him CPR. We don't yet know the damage, if any, to his heart."

"Oh, I pray he'll be all right. Thankfully your husband acted quickly."

"That's what the doctors are saying. He may have saved Harry's life."

"I should be there," Ali said, thinking aloud.

Judy didn't hesitate to reply. "Ali, I've never seen your mother so frightened and nervous. I tried my best to calm her down. Perhaps you should come."

"I'll take the red-eye. Please tell my mom that I'm on my way."

"I will. I know she needs you, Ali," Judy said. "She's trying to be so brave, but having you here would really help."

"I should be there early in the morning."

"I'll tell her you're coming. I think it's going to be a long night."

For both of us, Ali thought. She hung up and made reservations at Sacramento International Airport. Then she packed an overnight bag. If she left right now, she'd have just enough time to make her flight.

Ali waited until she checked in for her flight before calling Joe. She'd almost forgotten about him and their weekend plans. She couldn't imagine having Joe show up at her door in the morning and realize he'd been stood up. It was either that or calling him at midnight.

He answered on the third ring. "Hello," he grumbled, his voice raspy. It was clear that she'd woken him up. "Sorry to call so late, Joe."

"Ali?"

"Yes, it's Ali. I'm at the airport. My stepfather had a heart attack. I'm on my way now to be with him and my mom."

"Oh," he said, his voice sounding more alert now. "Sorry to hear that." He seemed a little confused.

"I'll be in Florida this weekend. Just wanted you to know in advance so you could cancel the bike tour for tomorrow. I'm sorry. I was really looking forward to it."

"Yeah, I was, too," he said. "But that can be rescheduled. You need to be with your family now, Ali."

Ali's heart surged. She didn't have much family, and she hadn't had a great childhood, but she loved her mother, even with her flaws. And she knew that she needed to be by Justine's side now. "I hope to be back by Monday."

"Don't worry about it. I can manage at the office without you for a few days," he said, and then added, "barely. Take the time you need."

Ali smiled for the first time since she'd seen that newscast on television tonight, and her mood lightened a bit. "Thank you, Joe."

"Have a good flight. I'll see you when you get back."

"Okay."

Ali hung up the phone, and her good mood immediately vanished. Oh, how she wished Joe were here, lending comfort and holding her, telling her it was going to be all right. How she longed to hear him say he loved her. The bike tour would have been a means for them to get closer, to spend time together outside of work.

Then a distressing thought struck. Could this be an omen of some kind? Maybe the deception and her plans to entice Joe into noticing her were backfiring. Maybe it just wasn't meant to be. After all, she was forcing every situation with Joe, and that's not how she normally operated.

Ali shoved those plaguing thoughts aside when she boarded the plane. She dozed during the flight, and before she knew it, she had arrived in West Palm Beach.

* * *

At precisely 9:00 a.m. Ali walked into the hospital, eager now to see her mother and praying that Harold had held on during the night.

"Ali!" Her mother dashed across the waiting room when she spotted her, tears flowing down her cheeks. Ali feared the worst.

When her mother reached her, she wrapped her arms around her and hugged her tight. "I'm so glad you're here."

"I am, too, Mom. How's Harold?"

Justine began crying again, and Ali walked her over to a bench seat and guided her down. Ali sat next to her and offered her a tissue. "He's holding on. I'm to blame for this. His heart attack is all my fault, Ali."

Ali's mother broke down, crying so hard, Ali had to hold her as if she were a baby. She cradled her in her arms and held her, rocking her back and forth. "No, Mom, it's not your fault. It's not."

"We were always arguing," she said between sobs. "I wouldn't give in."

"But that means he wouldn't give in either, right?"

"Right, but what if I caused this? What if…he dies? Oh, Ali. I couldn't live with myself."

Now was not the time for blame, and Ali understood that. "Let's hope he survives this, Mom. Then you both will have to change your ways. But let's not think about that. Let's focus our energy on Harold getting better."

"I just wanted him to slow down," her mother said quietly, her voice drifting. "We're not getting any younger, and I wanted him to stop working so much. He needed a vacation. We both did. It was the best advice, Ali. I finally got him to go on that cruise and we were having—" she stopped to take a breath and dab at her eyes with the tissue

"—we were having such a lovely time. We hadn't argued once on the yacht. Then all of a sudden, he collapsed, right there on the deck, and I thought he'd died."

"You got him help quickly. The senator might have saved his life."

Justine looked at her with soulful eyes. "I've been praying so hard for him, Ali. Lord, I love him so much."

Ali had never seen her mother react this way. Justine had always been indulged. Her husbands had spoiled her, and she'd relished their attention and gifts. In some ways, her mother had been selfish and self-indulgent.

But Justine Holcomb was a different woman now. Ali saw the truth in her eyes and heard the sincerity in her tone. Her mother had finally and fully fallen in love.

Ali's heart ached thinking her mom might lose Harold now, after she'd found the right man to share her life with. It had taken her five tries to do it and all those years of searching. Ali was convinced that her mother would fall apart if she lost her husband.

Though Ali would never want to walk in her shoes, she believed her mother was ultimately a good person. She refused to believe any of the hushed rumors that Justine was a gold digger.

She shuddered at the thought. It was such an ugly label.

"Mom, let's go grab a cup of coffee. I'm operating on a few hours' sleep."

Her mom nodded and they rose, Justine taking one quick look at the critical care room where Harold rested.

"C'mon, Mom. He's not alone. And I bet you've been in there all night with him. Let's get you some breakfast."

On Saturday, Joe rose early and swam his usual one hundred laps in the pool. He ate a breakfast of cooked oats, toast, eggs and orange juice on the patio then showered and dressed. Glancing at his watch, seeing the time approach when he would have been picking up Ali for their bike tour, disappointment registered.

He admitted how much he'd been looking forward to spending the day with her. He wondered how she was faring, taking the red-eye and flying across the continent in the middle of the night, not knowing what she'd find when she arrived. He realized he didn't really know much about Ali's family life. He'd never asked. Had she been close to her stepfather? How would she handle it if the worst happened?

Joe hoped, for Ali's sake, that she wouldn't have to deal with any loss. Having lost his mother and father, he knew firsthand about grieving and heartache.

He didn't want Ali to go through that alone.

Joe drove to the office and finished up some work he'd had to do. "Busy work," he muttered, staring at his computer screen after he'd accomplished his goal in thirty minutes.

He felt at loose ends today with thoughts of Ali never far from his mind. But Joe was resolute, if anything. His vow to keep his distance and not get involved with her was imperative to his sense of well-being. Unfortunately, he couldn't stop thinking about her. He'd glanced at the phone a half dozen times since walking into his office, tempted to call her.

But wouldn't she read something more into that than he intended?

When his phone rang, Joe's heart sped up. He grabbed his iPhone and quickly saw Tony's image pop up on the screen. He felt a measure of disappointment and almost laughed aloud at how ridiculous that was. Had he really thought Ali would call him? She'd barely been gone twelve hours.

"Grapes to grow," he answered.

Tony chuckled. "Wine to flow."

And Nick's line was always "Cash to blow." Typical of Nick, Joe thought. He shook his head. "I don't know why I said that."

"It's been years. Reminds me of high school."

"Yeah, the old man didn't appreciate our little jingle," Joe mused.

"He was more bark than bite. I'd catch him with a grin, when he thought I couldn't see him."

Joe surmised that people tended to remember the good about a person after they were gone, choosing to forget the bad.

"I thought I'd be speaking into your voice mail. Rena said you had a hot date with Ali today."

"Nothing hot about it, Tony. Unless you call a bike tour around Napa a big deal. Ali had an emergency last night. She flew to Florida."

"What kind of emergency?"

"Her stepfather had a heart attack."

"That's rough. How's he doing today?"

"I don't know. I haven't heard from her."

"You haven't called her?"

Joe inhaled sharply. "No."

Tony was silent for a few seconds. "Okay. So what are you doing today? Don't tell me you're at the office."

"Okay, I won't."

"Joe, you can't spend all your time there. Give yourself a break."

"Just clearing up some last-minute things." Joe didn't know why he had to defend his efficiency, yet both of his brothers taunted him about it, until they needed his help with something. Then, they praised his abilities and work ethic.

"Rena and I are coming into town for lunch. Why don't you join us?"

"Yes, join us," he heard Rena call into the phone.

"There," Tony said. "You can't very well refuse a pregnant lady."

"Well, in that case, sure. I'll have lunch with you."

"My wife's got a craving for Italian food. Meet us in a half hour at the Cordial Contessa," Tony said.

"I'll be there," he said.

Thirty minutes later, Joe strode into the quiet, dimly lit restaurant and found his brother nuzzling Rena's neck at a table set for three. "Maybe I should bow out gracefully and let you two get a room."

Rena chuckled and lifted her arms up in welcome. "Come here, Joe, and give your sister-in-law a hug."

After giving her a gentle embrace, he kissed her cheek. "It's good to see you, Rena." Then he turned to shake Tony's hand.

"I'm glad we dragged you outta that pit," his brother teased.

"You mean, the pit with state-of-the-art technology that keeps a roof over all of our heads?"

"The very one," Tony replied. "What brought you into the office today?"

"I'm finishing up a weekly accounting, that's all. Crunching numbers."

"What else is new." Tony looked at Rena and winked. "You need to get a life, Joe."

"I have a life. *A good life.* And I'm trying to keep it that way."

"Meaning?"

"I've been following current buying trends and working

up graphs. Even in today's lackluster economy, people are still drinking wine—to drown out their troubles, maybe. But sales are holding strong."

"That *is* good news," Rena said. "I'm happy to say that Purple Fields is holding its own, too." Rena glanced at the menu. "I'm famished. It all looks so good. Today, I'm going to eat for two and not feel guilty about it."

They gave their orders to the waiter, and the meal was delivered shortly after. They sat in silence for the most part, gobbling down their meals. The veal scallopini was the best Joe had ever had.

"Mmm," Rena said after finishing off her meal. She leaned back and patted her stomach. "So good."

"My pasta primavera was perfect," Tony said. "This place is giving Alberto's a run for the money."

"Yeah, why aren't we eating there?" Joe asked. The Carlinos owned half interest in an Italian restaurant that served Tuscany fare.

"My fault," Rena said with a quick smile. "After having this yummy lemon sesame chicken pasta dish at our reception, I've been craving it all week. The chef is a genius."

And just as she spoke of him, Royce walked out of the kitchen, holding a tray of pastries. "For the newlyweds," he said, placing the delicate tray onto the table. "I'm so happy you came to the Contessa for lunch."

"I told you we would," Rena said. "I've been craving this dish all week. Oh, and these pastries. I can't possibly pass them up."

Royce looked pleased. "Enjoy them."

"Thank you," Tony said.

Royce glanced at each of them. "Would any of you like some coffee?"

"I'm fine with water," Rena said.

"I'm fine, too," Tony added.

"No thanks," Joe said, inexplicably miffed that Royce had made such an impression on Rena and Tony.

"Royce," Rena began. "I know I told you this before, but I'm very glad Ali recommended you for our reception. Everyone complimented the food."

"That's very nice of you to say. Ali's been a good friend."

Rena nodded. "She's a special friend to me, too. I hope she's doing okay."

"She's fine. I spoke with her this morning."

Joe's head snapped up, and he narrowed his gaze on Royce. "How's her stepfather?" he asked. But what he really wanted to ask was why the *hell* did she call you?

"Out of danger, but looks like he'll have a long rehab period. Ali said her mom was really upset, but they are both relieved that he'll make a full recovery in time."

"Oh, that's good to hear," Rena said, glancing at Joe. She seemed to read his mind. "Did she say when she'd be coming home?"

"Probably in a few days. I'm picking up her mail and newspapers and watering her plants for her."

Joe sat there, keeping a steady noncommittal look on his face, while inside his gut churned. "I told her to take as much time as she needs."

"She's planning on calling you tomorrow."

Joe didn't want Royce's blow-by-blow accounting as to Ali's plans. The guy really irked him. Or rather, as Joe mulled it over methodically in his mind, Ali's relationship with Royce was the true source of his irritation.

He nodded and looked away.

"Well, I'd better get back in the kitchen. Enjoy the rest of your meal."

Once Royce walked away, Rena and Tony stared at him.

Joe adjusted his glasses on his nose then spoke when he couldn't ignore their stares another second. "What?"

Tony grinned. "You should see the look on your face. The Grinch has nothing on you."

"Tony," Rena said, grabbing his arm. "Let's drop it."

"Your wife is a smart lady," Joe said.

Tony aimed a headshake at him before digging into a raspberry tart. "Royce sure knows what he's doing," he added after he finished.

The hidden message in his brother's comment wasn't lost on him. "I told you I'm not interested in Ali."

"Who said anything about Ali?" Tony feigned innocence.

"Joe," Rena began. "I was hoping you could do us a favor. Tony and I were scheduled to go to San Francisco for the Annual Grapegrowers Convention. But I'm really feeling tired lately."

"You are?" Tony looked at her with surprise.

Rena turned to her husband and gave him a small smile. "I am, honey. I didn't want to worry you. It's just a combination of the pregnancy and not getting good sleep. I think the trip would exhaust me." She turned her attention toward him. "Would you mind going in our place?"

"You haven't missed that event since you took over Purple Fields," Tony said.

"I've never been pregnant before, either," Rena shot back a little too quickly. Joe had a sneaking suspicion this was a setup, but he couldn't refuse Rena the favor.

"I'll go. Don't worry, Rena."

"I know it's a lot to ask on short notice." Rena seemed really contrite.

Joe gestured away her worry. "I'll have help. I'll take along a secretary."

"That's a good idea," Rena said, seemingly satisfied.

"I think Jody Millwood might be available."

Rena's eyes went wide with shock, and Joe gave himself a mental pat on the back. Rena's expression spoke volumes. He knew what she was up to.

"The woman from your sales office?" Rena's voice elevated slightly. "She's…well, she's a bit—I think she spends her weekends with her grandchildren."

Grinning, Tony caught on and shook his head. "Sweetheart."

Joe frowned. "You two don't give up, do you?" He didn't give them time to protest. "You know what, if I take Ali to the convention and come out of it unscathed, then will you both get the message and quit matchmaking?"

Rena clamped her mouth shut and nodded.

Tony smiled.

"Fine, then," he said. "I'll hold you to your word."

Seven

On Sunday night, just as Joe was retiring for bed, his cell phone rang. He answered it and heard Ali's voice on the other end. "Hello, Joe. It's Ali." She sounded somber, so unlike herself.

"Ali? Are you okay?"

"I'm doing fine, I guess. Just a little tired." He heard the sigh in her voice and wanted to kick himself for not calling her. He glanced at the clock. It was after one in the morning in Florida. "I wanted you to know that I won't be coming back until Tuesday night. I'll take some personal time, if that's okay."

"Don't worry about that, Ali." Damn it, she sounded so businesslike, calling her boss to report her absence at work. Joe thought they'd progressed beyond that. "Take all the time you need."

"Thank you."

"How's your stepfather?"

"He's out of the woods, right now. There was some damage to his heart, but thankfully he'll recover with rehab and a lifestyle change."

"And how's your mother doing?"

"She was overwrought when I first got here, but she's doing much better now. She's taken hold of the situation, making plans for when Harold comes home and how things will change for the better. I'm really proud of her."

There was a lull, and Joe sensed Ali was ready to end the conversation. But he wasn't. He missed talking to her. During the past four weeks, they'd spent a lot of time together at the office and working on the wedding reception. He didn't like how he felt at loose ends without her. "What are you doing now? It's late there, isn't it?"

"Yes, it's past one. I'm getting ready for bed."

Joe's mind took a U-turn, envisioning her slipping off her clothes, donning a sheer nightie that would keep her cool in the humid Florida climate, her hair unrestrained and flowing in curls past her shoulders. He stifled a groan.

"What are you doing?" she asked softly.

"The same. Getting into bed." He flashed a vision of Ali joining him under the sheets and couldn't deny how much the thought pleased him.

"Sorry if I disturbed you."

"Not at all." He missed her. And it was on the tip of his tongue to say so. He should have called her. He should have at least expressed his concern for her stepfather and checked in on her. But his vow to steer clear of her had stopped him. "I'm glad you called."

"You are?" She sounded doubtful.

"The fact is," he began, fumbling with the right words to say, "it's good to hear your voice. I was concerned for you."

"Oh, well, I'm fine. I appreciate your concern."

Joe winced. They were speaking as if they were total strangers, their conversation stilted and deliberate. And had he heard a note of disappointment in her voice? Should he have said more? "I'd better let you get to sleep."

"You, too. Sleep tight, Joe."

He didn't know how much sleep he'd get, but one thing was certain—his entire body was as *tight* as a hangman's noose.

"Good night, Ali."

Frustrated, Joe climbed into bed, realizing his hands-off approach with Ali was backfiring. The more he kept to his resolve, the more he wanted her.

And this wasn't a problem he could solve with his unique mathematical skills.

As soon as the plane landed at Sacramento Airport, Ali grabbed her overnight bag and scooted down the narrow aisle, glad to be back in California. She'd had an exhausting four days and felt like the scourge of the earth in her clothes. She'd tossed together only one outfit change in her hurry to get to Florida, and she hadn't had time to do any laundry while she was there. The clothes on her back were beyond wrinkled.

Ali walked down the long corridor leading to the airport terminal, her body aching and her eyes burning from the little bit of sleep she'd gotten these past days. But the minute she glanced up and saw Joe, standing there waiting at the gate, a burst of stunned joy entered her heart.

He tipped his head when he spotted her. She'd never been so glad to see anyone in her life. Joe, with his hair slightly disheveled, wearing jeans and a black T-shirt, looking better than any of God's creations, was the one and only person who could lift Ali's spirits. She wanted to run to him with outstretched arms and kiss him silly.

But the new Ali would never do something like that. Fake Ali, as she called herself, would simply approach him with a smile, which was exactly what she did.

"Hi, Joe," she said, her breath nearly catching.

"It's good to see you, Ali."

She blinked and waited. Joe noted her hesitation. Then he opened his arms, and she walked straight into them. "Are you okay?"

She nodded, digging her head into his chest and holding on. Tears stung her eyes. She kept telling herself he'd never be here if she hadn't begun this ruse. Somehow that justified her actions. "How did you know what flight I was on?"

"I didn't. But this was the only evening flight coming in from Florida. It seemed logical."

God, how she loved him. "Thank you for coming. But I have my car here."

"Don't worry about your car. I'll have someone pick it up for you. I brought a limo. Thought you'd like a quiet drive home."

Ali nodded. "Sounds like heaven. This is very kind of you."

Joe squeezed her tight and then looked into her eyes. "You've had a rough few days, haven't you?"

Ali cringed. She must look awful. "Yes."

Joe hadn't called her during those four days, and as ridiculous as it seemed, her feelings had been hurt. She'd thought they were closer than that. She'd thought that Joe would have given her more support. Those few kisses they'd shared had given her hope, but she'd come to realize that maybe Joe would never come around. Not in the way she wanted.

"I'm sorry." There was a depth to his tone she hadn't heard before.

"Sorry?"

"That you had to go through that alone."

She shrugged. "At least, my mother is handling it better now."

"Thanks to you, Ali. I bet you being there meant the world to her. You have a way of making people feel better."

When Joe said things like that to her, it made her want to shed tears. He could be so sensitive at times. "I hope so."

Joe snatched her bag from her hand and guided her out to the parking lot. True to his word, a black limo was waiting with a chauffeur who had opened the door the minute he'd spotted Joe.

"After you," he said to her, then handed over her bag to the driver. Joe slid in beside her, and the door was closed.

Ali couldn't keep from asking, "I thought you were the green guy in the family."

Joe laughed. "I am," he said as if he'd just been caught cheating on an exam. "But some things are just worth the carbon footprint."

Ali smiled. "Thank you, Joe."

"Lean back and relax. You must be exhausted."

Ali did just that. She slid down in her seat a little and rested her head back. "Do I look that bad?"

"No, actually you look amazing."

She tilted her head to gaze at him. Those dark eyes behind the glasses appeared sincere. It was on the tip of her tongue to tell him how much she'd missed him, but Ali held back.

Joe slid a little closer and opened his arms to her. "Lean against me, and close your eyes."

The invitation was too tempting to refuse. Silently, she

did as she was told. The minute she rested her head on his chest and his arm wrapped around her, a sense of peace and fulfillment washed over her. "Mmm."

"Try to sleep," he whispered.

"You make the best pillow, Joe," she said, cuddling into him. "I think I will."

Ali knew the exact moment the limo rolled to a halt. Her eyes snapped open. Joe held her against him as she slept, and now she wished she hadn't woken up at all. She wished she could stay in his arms forever.

"You're home," Joe said quietly.

She *felt* at home in his arms. At least now, she could say she'd slept with Joe—or rather *on* him. She slid out of his grasp and straightened in her seat. Oh God, had she snored? "How long was I out?"

"Just about the entire way, Ali."

"Was I, um—"

"Peaceful. And quiet as a mouse."

Thank God. She blinked then nodded, trying to wake up fully.

"If you need another day to rest, take it."

"No," she said shaking her head. "I'm eager to get back to work. I, uh, missed it."

Joe smiled and looked deep into her eyes. "Good, because things don't run smoothly without you."

Ali searched his eyes. Should she read more into his compliment? "That's nice to hear."

The chauffeur opened the door on her side. "Well, this is my stop."

"I'll walk with you." Joe got out on his side of the limo, grabbed her overnight bag from his driver and then met up with her. They walked to her condo in silence. When she reached her front door, she turned to him. "Thanks for the ride. It meant a lot."

Joe searched her eyes and nodded. "You're welcome." He hesitated for a moment, then scratched his head and let go a deep sigh. "Ali, maybe now's not the best time to ask, but are you free this weekend?"

This weekend? Ali's sluggish body registered a happy alert. Was he going to reschedule their bike tour? There wasn't anything she had planned that she wouldn't cancel for him. "Yes, I think so."

"I'm afraid it's a working weekend in San Francisco. I'm elected to go to the Annual Grapegrowers Convention. Rena and Tony were planning on going, but Rena isn't up to it."

"So, they asked you to go?"

He nodded. "And I need your help, if you're willing to work the weekend."

Ali held her smile inside. An entire weekend in San Francisco with Joe? Every tired nerve in her body jumped for joy. This was a dream come true. "I can manage it. Sure, I'll go with you."

Joe seemed relieved. "I appreciate it, Ali. You never let me down."

Ali reached up and kissed him on the cheek. "Thanks again," she whispered, her breath caressing his throat.

Joe blinked and leaned closer, his intense gaze focused on her mouth.

Ali opened her door and slid inside, popping her head out. "I'll see you tomorrow."

She closed the door and held her breath. "Fake Ali," she muttered, "this better work because you just left the man of your dreams hanging outside your door."

Friday night hadn't come fast enough for Ali. She'd spoken with Rena out of concern for her well-being, only to have been assured that her pregnant friend was doing just fine. Rena confessed that begging off from this trip was a perfect way to get Ali together with Joe in a romantic setting. She'd been darn proud of her plan, and Ali had thanked her matchmaking friend.

Each day since Ali had returned to work she'd found Joe staring at her from his desk, his expression intense. The minute they'd make eye contact, Joe would glance away as if he'd been caught with his hand in the cookie jar. She'd been encouraged and at the same time, felt like a complete con artist, gaining his attention by deceptive means. The subdued hair, the glasses and the conservative clothes were everything she was not.

But now as Ali put her clothes on hangers, her room just a few steps away from Joe's in San Francisco's luxurious Four Seasons Hotel, hope filled her thoughts. She couldn't keep from smiling. Joe, the rock-solid man who held her heart, would be picking her up soon for the Welcome Dinner in the Grand Ballroom.

She knew Joe didn't like these stuffed-shirt affairs. Neither did she, really. Though she'd never have refused this invitation, she wished that they were here for a romantic weekend rather than rounds of business dinners and lectures. "A girl can only dream," she said softly.

She had just enough time to freshen up and dress before Joe would be knocking on her door.

Ali swept her massive hair back into a tight ponytail, allowing a few curly tendrils to fall demurely along her cheeks. She applied a light coat of makeup, just a hint of green shadow to bring out the color of her eyes and a soft peach lip gloss to tint her lips.

She slipped into a black chiffon dress that Rena helped her pick out for tonight's formal dinner. With a square neckline that dipped just a little below her throat, no one could accuse her of looking indecent. The bodice accented her narrow waistline then flowed in wispy folds to just above her knees. An antique pearl necklace complimented the dress and of course, Ali wore the diamond bracelet Joe had given her. She put her feet into two-inch black pumps and finished the whole look by putting on her glasses.

She glanced in the mirror. "You fraud," she whispered.

The knock at the door came precisely at seven o'clock.

Excitement coursed through her system. She dashed to the door, then remembered to compose herself, taking a steadying breath before opening it slowly.

When she glanced at Joe standing at her threshold in a black tuxedo, his dark hair smoothed back and curling at the base of his neck, his face tanned from morning swims and those dark eyes, intense once again, she might have swooned had she been faint of heart.

"You look very nice, Joe," she said quietly.

Joe's lips curved up in a killer smile. "Thanks. And you look beautiful tonight, Ali."

She did? She thought otherwise—the mundane dress was boring with a capital *B*. "Thank you."

"Are you ready to schmooze?"

Ali smiled. "As ready as you are."

Joe frowned. "Not the best way to spend your weekend, is it?"

Was he kidding? There was no place she'd rather be. Ali tilted her head. "I'll survive."

Once at the Welcome Dinner, Ali remembered that this was indeed a working weekend. She kept her eyes and ears open and networked with several winemakers along with Joe. They took their seats after the cocktail hour and listened to the keynote speaker's views on winemaking and the economy.

They dined at a table with three CEOs and their wives, Ali entering into light conversation with the women about West Coast versus East Coast fashions. Ali engaged them while Joe spoke with the men at the table, and after a sumptuous meal, all business was concluded.

A seven-piece orchestra began playing what Ali could only describe as nondescript music. The mellow tunes allowed for close proximity on the dance floor, and as men swept their partners to the center of the room, Ali found Joe deep in conversation with the head of Paladino Wines.

When she was tapped on the shoulder from behind, she turned to a man with hopeful eyes. "Would you care to dance?"

Ali hesitated for one second, glancing at Joe, who seemed oblivious to anything but the deep conversation he engaged in. She couldn't see refusing the middle-aged man, whose name tag revealed him to be a master sommelier. "Yes, thank you."

The man pulled out her chair and waited as she rose and headed for the dance floor. "My name is Juan Delgado," he said.

"Ali Pendrake."

He nodded with a smile and guided her to the dance floor, then took her into his arms as the music played on and literally swept her off her feet. Juan Delgado was not only a wine professional but a marvelous dancer.

Juan took dancing seriously, and there was no time for talking. Ali was curious about him, the man with kind eyes and exquisite dance steps. She'd never felt so weightless while dancing before.

"You dance with spirit, Ali," he said as the dance ended. "If I could confess, I'd love to dance with you all evening."

Juan continued to hold her waist, and his interest deepened to another level, one Ali recognized as dangerous. She glanced at her table and found Joe gone. Scanning the room, she locked gazes with him on the edge of the dance floor, his face tight, his body held in a rigid stance.

Ali had never seen that expression on Joe's face. Her pulse raced with dread. Had she done something wrong?

She turned back to Juan. "You're a wonderful dancer, Juan, and I did enjoy the dance, but I'm afraid I'm not here to dance. I must get back to my table. I'm…working."

"Aren't we all?" The casual tone in his voice belied the passion in his eyes.

Ali broke all contact with him. "Really, Juan. I have to go. Thank you for the dance."

Ali turned and walked straight into Joe, smacking into his chest. "Oh!"

He took her hand. "I need to speak with you," he said, leading her off the dance floor, then out of the ballroom entirely. Ali's heels scraped the floor trying to keep up.

Joe kept walking at a brisk pace, and Ali's mind whirled with confusion. Once he found a secluded alcove in the hallway, he pulled her inside and turned her, pressing her back to the wainscoted wall.

Ali had no time to react. Joe braced the wall behind her with both hands, brushed his hips against her, then crushed his mouth to hers, claiming her in an all-consuming kiss.

The kiss went long and deep, and tears of joy filled her closed eyes. Her mind screamed her love for him, her body turning to jelly in an instant.

Whatever this was, Ali had never experienced such intense passion. This kiss was urgent and fiery beyond her wildest dreams.

Joe didn't let her come up for air. He kissed her again and again, his musky scent filling her nostrils, his powerful body taking full control. Ali relished every second of his passion. Then finally, when both of them were ragged and nearly breathless, Joe broke away to look at her, his eyes gleaming with dark intensity.

"I like you, Ali."

"I like you, too, Joe."

"Wanna blow this damn convention?"

She thought he'd never ask. "Blow it?"

"I want you, Ali," he said, his voice a deep rasp.

Ali's brows rose in response.

He cupped the nape of her neck and eased her head back, planting tiny mind-blowing kisses along her throat. "I want to make love to you all weekend."

"Oh, Joe," she whispered. Her heart nearly burst from her chest.

"I don't want to see you in the arms of another man. I want that right for myself." His next kiss curled her toes. "You have to know I didn't plan this, but it's happening and I can't stop it."

"I know," she whispered. "I know. I don't want you to stop."

Joe gazed into her eyes for a brief moment and smiled. "Then let's go."

He grabbed her hand and led her to the elevator. They waited impatiently, and once the elevator dinged and the doors opened, Joe strode inside, punched the button and took her into his arms again. He kissed her like there was no tomorrow, and they were both breathless when they reached the sixteenth floor. Joe kissed her all the way to the room, both stumbling, and Ali thought she'd truly died and gone to heaven.

They fumbled with the keycard to open the door between kisses, and once inside, Joe shoved the door closed behind them. "I'm usually smoother than this."

Heart pumping like crazy, Ali smiled. "You're doing just fine."

Joe laughed. "Then in that case." He lifted her up in one fluid motion and strode into the bedroom. She wrapped her arms around his neck. Once he reached the king-size bed, he lowered her gently, and Ali released her hold on him.

He took his glasses off and then reached down to take hers off, as well. Then he pulled off the band that confined her auburn hair. He fingered through her tresses, watching the hair spread out across the pillow. "Amazing." He stood tall, straightening out, his gaze fixed on her. Loosening his tie, he removed his tux jacket and unbuttoned the first few buttons of his shirt.

Ali's breath caught. How many times had she dreamed of being with Joe like this?

Joe kicked off his shoes and joined her on the bed, crushing her again with kisses that left no room for doubt about where they were heading.

All the while, Ali held back. She wanted to strip Joe of his clothes, wiggle out of hers and unleash her own fiery passion. But Fake Ali couldn't do that. She had a role to play, and she reminded herself of the journey that had gotten her to this point.

Let it go, Ali. You're where you want to be.

Ali shoved her guilt and self-loathing out of her mind. With Joe beside her, it was easy to do.

He parted her lips and drove his tongue into her mouth. Ali let out a little moan of pleasure. The kisses went on and on until Joe's body went completely rigid with need.

He pulled away and yanked off his shirt, tossing it aside, then worked the back zipper of her dress. He eased it up and over her head, leaving her naked but for her black bra and bikini panties.

Joe took a good look and inhaled deeply, "Ah, Ali."

Ali gazed at him, consumed with love.

"You're beautiful."

So was he. His chest bare, she filled her gaze with broad shoulders, powerful arms and a ripped torso. Every ounce of her wanted to jump his bones right now, but Ali only reached for him and laid his hand on her breast.

Joe took it from there—his passion intensified, his eyes narrowed. The look he shot her was so steamy her insides melted.

He released her full breasts from their bonds and palmed her firmly, his hand rough against her soft skin. Next he grazed over her nipple, the tip pebbling hard. Over and over he touched her, his hand flat against her skin as he moved, explored, caressed and admired her body.

Her breaths shot out in short bursts, her pulse raced. "Oh, Joe," she murmured.

"Hang on, Ali." And before she knew it they were both fully unclothed. Joe slid his hands all over her naked body, kissing her senseless. Gliding his hand lower, anticipation built and every nerve ending tingled with intense awareness. This is the moment she'd wanted for so long—the moment when she and Joe would come together.

He cupped her between the legs and touched her gently at first, then with more and more intensity. Fireworks shot off in her head, and she moved under his ministrations. He stroked her like he would a keyboard with quickness and efficiency, his fingers masterful.

Ali returned his kisses, moved in harmony with him and clung to him as he lifted himself over her. Protection—that had almost magically appeared—was fixed in place. He spread her legs apart.

Ali held her breath and welcomed him with an arch of

her back. And then Joe was joined with her, his erection full and thick, driving into her with a slow deliberate thrust.

Joe's body shook. A low guttural groan of pleasure released from his throat. The union brought tears to Ali's eyes. Then she forgot all else as Joe deepened his thrust, filling her full.

He cursed, and she knew it was from the sheer awe of satisfaction he experienced. She felt it, too. Nothing in her life would ever compare to this.

He gazed down at her, and she curved her lips in a smile of encouragement. Then Joe let loose, his thrusts quick and fiery. He braced his hands on her hips and lifted her even higher, his body coated with moisture, his expression beautifully intense.

Ali relished his lovemaking, moving with him and enjoying each bit of stirring pleasure he brought her. She gave him full command of her body. His stamina amazed her, and she thought of all those early-morning workouts in the pool.

Ali's body reached an explosive point, and she threw her head back and arched way up, letting go of her control. Her release came in exquisite short bursts of surrender. She huffed out quiet little moans and looked up at Joe.

Controlling his own need, he held back until she'd been fully sated. Then his pace and rhythm changed to a frenzied assault, his thrusts hard and demanding until he, too, met with a powerful orgasm.

She watched his face change, his passion release and his body contract. It was stunning and magnificent, and Ali was sure she'd never witnessed anything so inspiring.

Joe eased down onto her, taking her head in his hands, and kissed her soundly. "Did I mention how much I like you?"

"You mentioned that," Ali answered with a chuckle.

Joe rolled off her, and her heated body cooled considerably without him. He turned toward her, his head braced on his hand. He seemed to have something on his mind. Ali recognized when he was in deep concentration. Then he blinked and shot her a serious look. "Stay with me tonight."

The only way she'd leave is if he threw her out. "Yes."

Joe took her into his arms, and they lay in silence together. Shortly after they climbed under the sheets, Joe fell asleep first and Ali watched him take deep breaths, wrapped in his arms.

She wished every night could be this perfect.

Eight

Joe's natural alarm clock woke him at six in the morning to the soft sound of Ali breathing. Her back was toward him, and the uniquely feminine curve of her body next to his was a sexy sight to behold. Her hair fell in wispy waves past her shoulders. On impulse, Joe reached out and touched a few strands, curling his fingers into the thick locks.

He closed his eyes and breathed in her scent.

He hadn't wanted this to happen. He'd fought it with all of his might, telling himself she was off-limits. And he'd been immune to her for a long while, looking at her through eyes that had once been deceived by a gorgeous face and killer body. He'd associated Ali with Sheila, perhaps unfairly, and he didn't want to go down that road of employer/employee ever again.

As a defense mechanism, Joe had dismissed Ali in his mind as nothing more than his very loyal business associate.

Then something changed.

Ali had changed, and he began viewing her differently. The changes in her weren't subtle, and he hadn't figured them out entirely. But Ali had become important to him—and not just because of how well they worked together.

Her neighbor Royce had given him a nudge, the irritating man who had more than friendship on his mind. Then last night, as she danced with her partner, who had all the grace of a swan, another man had approached Joe and asked if Ali was unattached.

"Is she fair game?" Those were the man's exact words.

Joe shot the guy a hard look, deciding right then and there that he couldn't let Ali go. He'd booted the man with a cold and foreboding "no" and claimed her the moment the dance ended.

Joe nibbled on her shoulder, impatient for her to wake up, and when she turned around, he wasn't disappointed. Her green eyes sparkled when she gazed at him, the light in those orbs as brilliant as the sun.

He smiled. "Good morning, beautiful."

Ali's grin went wide, then as abruptly as she'd brought it on, she pulled back on her smile. The light in her eyes faded. "Good morning, Joe."

They'd had an incredible night of lovemaking, yet all the while, Joe felt something was wrong. Not that he could call her on it. He wasn't going to look a gift horse in the mouth. He was where he wanted to be, in bed with an intelligent, gorgeous woman.

He caressed her arm, gliding his hands up and down. "How did you sleep?"

"Very well. You?"

"I always sleep well. But this morning, I woke up and there you were. Sorry, but I couldn't keep from touching you." He leaned closer and kissed her. "You okay with this?"

Ali smiled again, and Joe felt better seeing genuine joy on her face. "I'm great with this."

She turned and braced up on her elbow, her hair flowing over her bare shoulder. She painted a lovely picture draped in the sheets. He could go on looking at her, but when the sheet slipped down and exposed her full breasts, his body reacted instantly.

She covered up, almost shyly, and Joe's sanity returned. "Ali, listen. I don't know where this is going and I want to be fair to—"

"Shh," she said, pressing two fingers to his mouth. "Joe, let's not analyze this. If this is only for the weekend then I'm good with that. And if Monday comes and we have to go back to business as usual, I'll be fine."

Joe took all of that in, wondering if he'd misunderstood her the other night when she'd told him she didn't do one-night stands—not that Joe wanted that with her anyway. He realized he was ready for more. Maybe even a relationship with Ali.

It'd be tricky at work, but they'd find a way.

"And what if we don't?"

"Don't?" she asked.

"Don't go back to business as usual?"

The brightness in Ali's eyes returned full force, transforming her expression into one of pure joy. "I could manage that, too."

Purposely now, she let the sheet slide lower down, and Joe's mind went on temporary vacation. He kissed her on the lips then rolled them both until she was under him. "How am I going to see you at work and not think of you like this?"

Ali pressed her hands to his chest. Oh God, it felt so

damn good. He wished she'd done more of that last night. "I could ask you the same question."

Joe wanted to make love to her slowly, leisurely this time, and devour every inch of her body. He wanted to kiss her into oblivion and then bring them both to simultaneous satisfaction.

But all of that would have to wait. "We can't do this anymore," he said, climbing off her.

Ali appeared stunned. "The convention?"

"Hell no," Joe said, unable to hide his smile. "We're blowing it off, remember?"

"Then?"

"I need to make a trip to the hotel gift shop. I told you I didn't plan any of this. I'm out of protection."

Ali nibbled on her lower lip in that adorable way of hers. Then she smiled. "I'll be waiting."

"Sleep, Ali. I'll take my swim, make that pit stop and be back here before you know it. I'll send up breakfast."

Joe rose from the bed and then leaned down to kiss her again. She watched him move around the room bare naked, her eyes softly following him, and that was enough to send his wicked mind into overdrive.

He dressed into swim trunks, threw his arms into a shirt and headed out. His mind conjured images of Ali waiting for him in bed. It was damn hard to leave her.

Doing one hundred laps in the hotel's junior Olympic-size pool would be his only salvation.

He needed a cold splash of reality.

Ali rested her head against her pillow and sighed. Blissfully happy, she thought about the past twenty-four hours. Joe had finally come around, but was the cost of his ardor too high? She didn't have an answer, and right now, maybe she shouldn't care. All of her dreams were coming true.

Too restless to lie there, Ali rose from bed and realized all of her clothes were still in her hotel room. She donned the dress she wore last night, finger-combed her hair, slipped her feet back into her pumps and left the room.

Once she got to her hotel room, just steps down the hall, she flopped onto her bed, in a quandary. "What now?"

She didn't want Joe to come back and find her gone. She would love to dress in her sexiest lingerie and seduce him the minute he returned to his room. The whole scene played out in her mind in erotically vivid details.

But that wasn't in the plan. And she couldn't tempt fate. The woman Joe was attracted to wouldn't take the reins like that. She wouldn't be the aggressor and let loose. It saddened her to think that Joe might never be attracted to the Real Ali.

She'd give him more credit than that but for the fact that they'd worked together for one year and the Real Ali had never interested him. She'd fallen in love with her boss, and he'd never known it. He wouldn't allow himself to see the truth, much less give the idea any credence at all. He'd had his heart broken by a woman who'd worked for him, and he wasn't going there again. She understood that.

Ali glanced at the digital clock. She didn't have much time. She rose and quickly showered then dressed in a pair of slacks and a soft scoopneck knit top. She pulled her hair back and put on her fake eyeglasses.

She entered Joe's room, and shortly after, room service knocked. She let the waiter in and watched as he set up the table by the large bay window. The food smelled wonderful, and Ali's stomach growled.

Joe walked in just as she nibbled on toast and sipped orange juice. "Hi," she said. "How was your swim?"

He swept into the room, looking magnificent, his dark hair wet and curling at the nape of his neck, his shirt rumpled and buttoned up only partway. Glancing at the clothes she'd put on, he tossed a bag onto the nightstand then strode over to her. "Too long." He bent down to take her face into his hands. Searching her eyes first, he brushed his lips to hers. "I missed you. Couldn't you sleep?"

"No, I, uh…I couldn't." She was still recovering from Joe's admission that he'd missed her. "I didn't have any clothes and with room service coming—"

"It's okay, Ali." He kissed her deeply this time, his mouth making love to hers in a slow deliberate way that curled her toes. Her mind went on autopilot, and she returned his kiss. She was becoming accustomed to Joe kissing her, taking liberties that only made her love him more.

"You should have seen the look on the clerk's face when I walked in dripping wet and bought condoms."

Ali laughed. "I wish I'd been there." Then she thought about it. "On second thought, no, I don't."

Joe grinned. "No, I guess you don't." He lifted the covers from the food plates and seemed satisfied with what he found. "Go on and eat if you're hungry. I'll take a quick shower and be right back."

"I'll wait for you," she said softly. "We'll eat together."

Joe inhaled and peered at her as if she'd granted him knighthood. "Thanks. I won't be long."

Ali heard the shower going on, and all sorts of erotic images played out in her mind. She imagined steamy water raining down his body, his skin sleek and slippery as he soaped up.

Ali rose from the table and peered out the window, trying to thwart her wayward, X-rated mind. The view from the sixteenth floor was inspiring. She wrapped her arms around her middle and enjoyed the rise of the sun over the

Pacific Ocean. The San Francisco Bay was a sight she'd only seen on postcards.

"I'll take you wherever you want to go today." From behind, Joe put his hands on her shoulders and planted little kisses on the nape of her neck.

Goose bumps rose up her arms from the thrill. He smelled fresh and clean, the subtle scent of lime on his skin.

Could she tell him she only wanted to see him between the sheets again? "I'll go wherever you want to take me, Joe."

Joe chuckled. "Then we won't get very far."

She turned around in his arms and stared into his eyes. "Oh, no?"

"The bedroom beckons, Ali." Then he gestured to the table. "And so does the food. C'mon," he said, taking her hand. It was only then she realized he had nothing on but a fluffy white towel around his waist. How would she get through the meal? "I know you're hungry. Sit," he ordered. "Eat up."

"Yes, boss."

Joe squeezed his eyes shut. "Ouch. Let's forget I'm your boss this weekend."

She wanted to ask him, but then who are you? My boyfriend? My lover? But Ali was too distracted by his ripped upper body to formulate any questions. And his lower body and the pleasures he'd evoked last night made her head swim. "I can do that."

She sat down and he joined her, sitting across the table. She had the most appealing view of a nearly naked Joe with San Francisco's famous skyline in the background. A girl couldn't ask for more.

Joe waited for her to fill her plate before he took his share. They dined on eggs Benedict, roasted potatoes and crepes with fresh summer fruit compote. The coffee was heavenly.

Once they finished the meal, Joe rose from the table and reached for her hand. She lifted up and stood before him, puzzled by the solemn look on his face. "I'm not the crafty old lecher trying to seduce my hot secretary, Ali, but I'd be lying if I said I didn't want to make love to you again."

Ali gulped air. She knew what Joe was trying to say. "I'm not doing anything I don't want to do, Joe. As far as I'm concerned, the sights in this room are pretty darn appealing. I don't need anything else."

He drew her in slowly, placing both hands on her waist. "I know how to compromise. We'll do a little of both. Well," he amended, "we'll do a *lot* of exploring in here and some exploring out there."

He sealed the deal with a long, lazy kiss. "How does that sound?"

Explore away, Joe, and leave no stone unturned, she wanted to say. "Wonderful."

Joe led the way, removing her clothes between kisses, and once inside the bedroom, he backed her up against the bed. They fell down together amid laughter, and Joe took his sweet time, discovering all of Ali's erotic zones.

He stroked her throat, tonguing his way up to her chin. Then he kissed her again and again in a sensual frenzy of lips and tongues. His hands inched their way down, and he caressed her breasts, flicking the tips until she bit down with silent urgent need.

Next, he traveled farther down, kissing her torso, her hips, her navel, gently easing his way lower. When he parted her legs and positioned himself, raising her hips to meet his mouth, he made love to her soft folds, until she nearly melted on the spot.

Joe didn't let up. He touched her everywhere, his hands roaming over her skin as he whispered soft endearments, his words muddling in her mind. He stroked her legs and arms with the same heat and passion, and once she was certain he'd caressed her everywhere, he stroked her apex again and again, this time pressing his palm against her silken, needy flesh.

"Joe," she huffed out, holding back her innermost desire to unleash her passion.

Joe removed his towel, and she watched as he rose above her like a magnificent animal ready to claim his mate. He was so beautiful that she wanted to cry.

Then he made love to her, entering her body and deepening his place in her heart. He owned her soul, and there was nothing she could do about it.

After, they stayed in bed and munched on the leftovers from breakfast, then on each other again. Morning became afternoon, and after they'd dozed in each other's arms for a few hours, she heard Joe stir beside her.

She opened her eyes to find him stretched out before her, his hands clasped behind his head. He'd put his glasses on, and the sexy picture he made with the silken sheet draped across his lower body and a look of pure contentment on his face, stole Ali's breath.

"It's almost three," he said.

Was that a hint for her to leave? She wasn't sure where she stood with him. They'd had hot sex, but he hadn't made any declarations to her other than soft stirring murmurs during the throes of passion. "Hmm. I guess I should go."

Joe turned to her. Shaking his head, his voice soft but commanding. "You're not going anywhere. I'll have your bags sent to my room. I want you here with me."

It was music to her ears.

"Don't you want that, too?" He draped his arm around her shoulder. She snuggled closer.

"Yes, of course I do."

"Look," he began, "I don't know where this is going, but I do know I don't want to waste a minute of this weekend without you. It's been a long time since—"

She lifted her head up to peer at him. "Since?"

"Since I've let myself get involved with anyone."

"Why?" Ali asked, though she suspected she knew the truth.

"Because I was engaged once, and to say it didn't work out would be an understatement."

"Tell me, Joe. What happened?"

Joe looked deep into her eyes with reluctance and regret. Through pain and anger, he admitted, "She wasn't the woman I thought she was."

Ali's heart plummeted. She was filled with dread and self-loathing at her own deception.

"I really loved her, or I thought I did at the time. A man has to think he's in love to offer marriage. It's only logical, right?"

"Right," Ali agreed, her pulse pounding.

"Ali, she worked for me before you came to Global."

He looked at her with guilt as if he'd done something unimaginable, while she was the true guilty one who was playing a dangerous game. "Go on."

"I should have never let it happen. She was a flashy woman, and I knew she was high maintenance when I got involved with her. I should have known better. She wanted me to change. To be someone I'm not. She thought after we got engaged that she'd be able to make me into someone more like Nick, for lack of a better example.

"The truth is, she wanted someone who liked to play at life, someone who tossed his money and power around to climb some sort of social ladder. Well, you know, I'm the green guy in the family. That's just not my thing. When she figured out that it wasn't going to happen, she found someone else. She left me for a wealthier, more powerful man."

"She broke your heart."

"I'm over it now. Have been for a long time."

"Oh, Joe, I'm deeply sorry." Ali meant it. She hated that Joe's heart had been broken, but at the same time she prayed that she wasn't going to do the same thing to him. Her deception haunted her, and she hated the weakness in her that caused her to lie to the man she adored, over and over again.

"I hope not too sorry?" He grinned and caressed her arms until she could barely think coherently.

"What do you mean?"

"You wouldn't be here with me if—"

"Oh." Then she smiled, too. "Yeah, I'm not *that* sorry."

Joe kissed her into oblivion, and she forgot all about her deception, his ex-fiancé and his heartbreak.

Nine

On Sunday morning, Joe took Ali to Chinatown, and as they strolled along the streets hand in hand, window-shopping, Joe found pleasure in buying Ali trinkets that sparked her interest. He held a shopping bag full of hand fans, embroidered handkerchiefs and little China dolls. He'd noticed Ali admiring a jade necklace, the delicate round disk an image of a Chinese garden, and he'd gone back to the store to purchase it.

"Oh, Joe," she said, with surprise in her voice. "I didn't expect you to—"

"I know, Ali. But I saw how much you liked it. I wanted you to have it."

Tears filled her eyes. "Thank you." She held the necklace to her chest. "I'll cherish it forever."

Joe took her hand, touched by her genuine appreciation, and they continued to stroll along. He spotted a shop selling hand-painted tea sets and tugged her along. "You have to have one," he said.

Ali shook her head. "No, Joe." She stopped on the street. "You've already given me too much."

Joe turned to her and cocked his head to one side. "Not as much as you've given me, honey."

And Joe realized the truth of that statement. He couldn't remember a time when he'd been so content. Ali had restored his faith in the opposite sex. He trusted her. They were compatible on every level. She was a decent, hardworking woman who didn't have an agenda where he was concerned.

"What have I given you?" she asked, puzzled.

Joe grinned. "A real good reason to get up and go to work every morning."

Ali let go a little gasp of surprise. "Joe."

"It's true. Now, c'mon. I want to show you the Golden Gate Bridge before lunch."

When they returned to the hotel room after lunch, Joe closed the door behind him and took Ali in his arms from behind. He pressed his body to hers and relished how right it felt to be near her. He kissed the back of her neck. "It was a good weekend." Then a chuckle escaped. "I dreaded coming here. I hate these things. But it turned out almost perfect."

Ali questioned him with a look. "*Almost* perfect?"

Joe nibbled on her neck some more. "You never invited me into your shower," he murmured.

Ali turned around in his arms and gazed deep into his eyes. "You don't need an invitation."

Joe raised his eyebrows. "I don't? Well then, I think you need a shower, Ali. You really worked up a sweat this morning." He sniffed the air around her playfully. "Yes, definitely. Oh, man, you really need to get clean."

Ali turned away from him and headed straight into the bedroom, kicking off her shoes and shedding clothes as she went.

Joe swallowed hard, watching her strip out of her clothes quietly. When she reached the master bathroom, he heard the shower door open then close and water rain down. He wasted no time yanking off his clothes and following her.

He joined her in the shower seconds later, and the sight of her, her hair wet and straight, hanging past her shoulders, her eyes brilliantly green and her body glistening with moisture, stole all of Joe's breath. "I wish we'd thought of this sooner. You're beautiful," he said. "Need some help?"

Ali handed him the bar of fragranced soap. Joe made a thick lather in his hands and stepped behind Ali. Winding his arms around her, he pressed the lather gently to her arched throat, then down along her shoulders, stroking her softly as his body became rock hard. Next, he slid his hands lower, soaping up under her arms and sliding his hands just under her ribs. Her intake of breath amplified his desire. He cupped her breasts, filling his hands with her weight, lathering her in circular motions, giving each perfect globe his undivided attention.

Ali moaned softly as he caressed her. She arched toward him, her body fitting his frame. His lust became almost tangible, his erection straining against her.

Joe spent a good deal of time massaging Ali, teasing and tormenting her breasts until she squirmed under his ministrations and huffed out deep breaths.

Joe was in no better shape. He was ready for more. He slid his hands lower, soaping her navel and just below. Steam built up in the shower, but nothing clouded Joe's vision of Ali, in his arms, bending to his will, allowing him the freedom to bring them both immense pleasure.

Joe cupped her between her legs, and she parted them, her moans of ecstasy mingling with his whispered demands. "Let go, baby. Let it happen."

He stroked her over and over, her body gyrating with his, his finger finding her core and breaching it. Beating rapidly, she moved with him, but Ali held back. He felt her control tight and sure.

Joe wanted to see her release, to see her relinquish that control and let go.

When she called his name like a plea, Joe's control snapped. There was only so much he could endure before realizing his own satisfaction. And Ali had him at his limit.

Joe moved against the thick shower glass and grabbed Ali's hips, sliding a hand along her back, bending her slightly. He leaned over her and cupped her breasts, then entered her soft folds from behind. She accommodated his body and both made quick adjustments to this new position. Then Joe drove a little deeper, holding Ali tight, their bodies joined in an erotic stance that heightened his pleasure even more.

He thrust slowly, deliberately, and Ali's body moved with him in a sensual rhythm. He slid his hand down to torment her most sensitive spot, his fingers urging her to completion as his thrusts grew more rapid, more demanding.

Joe kissed her shoulders, murmured loving words and moved with quicker strokes now, his body at its brink.

"Joe, now. Now," she rasped.

The soft flesh of her buttocks against his groin driving him crazy, he gripped her hips and pulled her against him. He drove deeper into her and split them both in two. Her release matching his, they moved in sync, Joe enjoying every movement, every gyration, until both were spent and fully sated.

They stayed in that erotic position until they caught their breath, then Joe whipped Ali around in his arms. When she wouldn't look into his eyes, he tipped her chin up and kissed her, wondering about her sudden shyness. She puzzled him in many ways, but all that was forgotten when she finally looked at him. Her gorgeous green eyes appeared soft and vulnerable, and a sudden flash jolted him. He was smart enough to realize that what he had with Ali wasn't just about sex.

He cared for her.

Deeply.

And he knew he was in trouble.

Joe left a sizable tip for housekeeping in his suite and then tipped the bellboy with a twenty after he'd brought their bags down to the lobby of the hotel. With Ali by his side, he'd never felt more content, and the staff was reaping the benefits of his good mood. The truth was that he hated to see the weekend come to a close.

As they waited for the valet to bring his car around to the front of the hotel, a familiar voice called to him.

"Joe! Joe, is that you?"

Joe turned around, and his good mood vanished when Sheila Maxwell, his ex-fiancée, strode up, her blond waves bouncing off her shoulders. She walked like a fashion model, her clothes Beverly Hills classy, white on white, and no one could miss the diamonds dripping from her ears and throat.

"Hello, Sheila."

Sheila walked up to him and kissed him on the cheek. "It's good to see you, Joe." She glanced at Ali with assessing eyes before turning back to him.

"This is Ali Pendrake." Joe felt obligated to introduce the women. "Ali, this is Sheila Maxwell."

"Sheila Desmond now," she corrected. "It's nice to meet you, Ali. What are you both doing here? Are you vacationing like I am?"

Ali hesitated, looking to Joe before answering. "No, we're here on business. There's a convention in town."

"Oh, right, the Annual Grapegrowers Convention. I'd heard it was at this hotel. Sorry, I didn't put two and two together. So, you work with Joe in Napa?"

"Yes, I do."

"Ali works for Carlino Wines, and we're lucky to have her," Joe added.

Sheila pursed her lips briefly, looking intently at Ali before focusing her attention back to him. Genuine sympathy softened her eyes, "I'm sorry about your father, Joe. I sent you a note of condolence. Did you ever get it?"

Bumping into Sheila after all this time confirmed Joe's suspicions that he was one hundred percent over her. He decided to put the past behind him. "Yes, I did. Thank you for that."

"So now, you're settled in Napa?"

"For the time being, I am. My brothers and I are running Carlino Wines now." He didn't give her an in-depth explanation. At one time, he'd shared everything with her.

The valet approached Joe, signaling to him. "Well, looks like my car is ready. It was nice talking to you."

"Uh, Joe. If I could have a minute of your time?" She searched his eyes, and he couldn't fathom what she wanted to say to him.

He pushed his glasses farther up his nose. "We really have to get going."

"It'll just take a minute. Would you excuse us, Ali?"

"No," Joe said immediately, glancing at Ali. "You don't have to—"

Ali put her hand on his arm briefly, a gesture Sheila didn't miss. "It's okay, Joe." She reassured him with a smile. "I'll wait in the car."

Joe furrowed his brows and watched her walk off. Then he turned his attention to his ex-fiancée, his annoyance barely hidden. He exhaled and waited.

"She's pretty."

"You didn't ask for privacy to tell me how pretty my assistant is."

"Is that all she is to you? Your assistant?"

"That's none of your business, is it?"

Sheila picked up on his brisk tone. "Listen, Joe, I'm not trying to cause any trouble for you. But as soon as I recognized her—"

"Who, Ali?" Puzzled, Joe frowned. "You know her?"

"Not personally, no. But I know the name, and I've met her mother, Justine. She's known in social circles as the beauty queen, and Ali is the spitting image of her."

Joe jammed his hands in his pockets. "Is there a point to all this?"

"I'm trying to warn you, Joe. Look, I don't want to dredge up past history or anything, but I know I hurt you. I'm deeply sorry about that."

Again, Sheila seemed contrite, which in itself, baffled him. "It's over and done with, Sheila."

"My point is that I don't want you to get hurt again. Ali's mother has dumped more men than a dog's got fleas. Did you know she's on husband number five?"

Joe didn't know that. In fact, every time he tried to ask Ali about her family and her childhood, she evaded the question. He'd figured she didn't like to talk too much about herself.

He remained passive, yet his curiosity was piqued.

"Not to mention how many boyfriends she's had in between her marriages. Each time she married, it was to a wealthier, more powerful man. She's married to Harold Holcomb now. His brother is a senator," Sheila added.

"I know that."

"Okay, just so you know. Justine Holcomb is a social climber. Some have been bold enough to call her a gold digger. Consider yourself warned. You know what they say—the apple doesn't fall far from the tree."

Joe almost laughed. If he wanted to use a cliché, something Sheila was famous for, he'd say her comment was like the pot calling the kettle black. "I've never met Ali's mother, and I'm not going to judge her behavior. But if you're insinuating that Ali Pendrake is going to hurt me, then I'd say you're wrong."

"Okay, Joe," Sheila said on a sigh. "I get it. I'm sorry for intruding. But just remember what I told you. Be careful."

"I'm always careful now. You taught me that."

Sheila blinked.

"Sorry," he said immediately. He'd never been one to retaliate, and oddly enough, he really believed that Sheila had no ill intentions toward him. She was way off base about Ali, though. He surmised that Sheila felt compelled to warn him, out of guilt.

She shook her head amiably. "No, it's probably the truth. I can't fault you for that. But I truly never intended to hurt you, Joe. And if it's any consolation, I'm happy. I'd like to see you happy, too."

"Don't worry about me. Look, I've got to run, Sheila."

"It was nice seeing you, Joe. Take care."

"Same to you," he said, backing away and turning toward the hotel doors. As much as he hated to admit it, Sheila had given him a good deal to think about on the ride back to Napa.

Ali should have been on cloud nine as they drove home from San Francisco. As far as weekends went, she'd never had a better one. The only flaw in her perfect adventure happened at the end of the day, as they were leaving the hotel. What were the chances that they'd come face-to-face with Joe's ex? Yet, there she'd been, holding his attention, looking beautiful.

Sheila had flair. She wore expensive clothes, had perfect hair and makeup and held herself with self-assurance. The twinge of jealousy that Ali felt when Joe introduced them couldn't be helped. Joe had been in love with her once. He'd wanted to spend the rest of his life with her. But it was more than that.

Sheila reminded her of someone. She seemed so familiar. And when it dawned on her, Ali bit down on her lower lip, squeezing her eyes shut. A sense of dread coursed through her system.

She's you, Ali. The Real Ali. The one Joe Carlino had refused to notice.

He'd wanted no part of someone who reminded him of the woman who'd broken his heart. Though Rena had spoken of it, Ali hadn't been quite sure, until she'd seen the woman for herself. It wasn't only that Joe shied away from office romances but it was because Ali had seemed too much like Sheila for him to give her a chance.

Ali snapped her eyes open and glanced at Joe. He was driving his hybrid car down the highway, deep in thought.

A million thoughts flooded her head as Joe remained

overly quiet for the rest of the trip home. Had seeing his ex jarred him? Was he still in love with her?

Oh, my gosh, Ali thought. *I'm the rebound woman and a fake one at that.*

Joe caught her staring at him. He cast her a thoughtful look, then reached for her hand. Entwining his fingers with hers, she felt somewhat better.

"Everything okay?" he asked.

"Everything's fine."

No. No. No, she wanted to scream. I need to know what Sheila really said to you. I need to know if you still love her. Joe's explanation when he got into the car at the hotel hadn't seemed plausible.

"She just wanted to make sure I wasn't holding a grudge," he'd said.

And Fake Ali hadn't probed him for more. She'd merely sat back in her seat and accepted his explanation. The whole way home Ali held her tongue, refraining from asking the questions she had every right to ask.

When they reached her apartment, Joe got out of the car and opened the door for her. He helped her out and then grabbed her bag from the trunk. He took her hand and led her up the path to her front door.

"Here we are," she said, needlessly. She turned to face him.

Joe looked deep into her eyes, removed his glasses, then removed hers and planted a kiss on her to end all kisses. Ali had barely come up for air when Joe kissed her again.

Wow.

Maybe she'd misread him before.

He held her close and nuzzled her neck. "I'm leaving. If I don't, I'd want to stay."

"And I'd want you to," she whispered.

He inhaled sharply and backed away. "It was a great weekend."

"It was," she agreed.

He stared at her mouth, then backed up some more. "I'm going now. I'll have all night to figure out how I'm going to keep my hands off you tomorrow at work."

Ali smiled. "Joe."

"Gonna be a long night." He scanned her body up and down. "A long night," he repeated.

Stay, she wanted to say. Stay and make love to me until the sheets catch fire. But Ali knew they'd have to get back to reality. They'd have to come to grips with their relationship—whatever it was.

"I'll see you tomorrow, Joe. I had a wonderful time."

She turned and entered her home, part of her wanting to jump for joy and part of her ready to shed worrisome tears.

Joe started work early on Monday morning. He'd had a poor night's sleep and figured why not put his energy into something productive. He had Ali on the brain and wondered about Sheila's accusations about her mother. It would be easy to find out more by looking her up on the Internet. He was certain Google wouldn't fail him, but Joe held off. He'd already decided to put no credence in Sheila's comments.

Ali wasn't like her mother, just like Joe wasn't like his father.

Sometimes the apple *did* fall far from the tree.

Joe dug into his work with added ambition, trying hard to concentrate on the task at hand. But the fresh scent of flowers drifted by his nose, and he knew the exact moment Ali had entered the office.

She popped her head inside his doorway, just like she'd done every other day. "Morning, Joe."

Joe sat back in his chair, glad to see her. "Good morning," he said, unable to hide a big smile, but before he could summon her inside, Ali was gone.

"Good thing," he muttered. He'd missed her soft, supple body next to his last night. It had been fantastic waking up with her in the morning and holding her in his arms while in San Francisco. He fought the urge to spend last night with her, because he wasn't sure where it would all lead. An open office romance could spell disaster if it didn't work out. He and Ali had such a fabulous work relationship, and he wanted to keep it that way.

He'd have to be content seeing her after hours, but that didn't stop his imagination from flashing images of hot office sex with Ali that would put his other sexual fantasies to shame.

This morning, he'd lost count during his swim somewhere after twenty-seven laps from thinking of Ali. For a man who banked on his analytical mind, that wasn't a good thing.

Joe ran figures of monthly sales on his computer, getting lost in numbers, but every once in a while, he'd hear Ali's voice as she spoke with a coworker and he'd look up. He found himself staring at her, his heart doing crazy little flips and his body growing tight.

She looked so studious in her glasses, with her hair pulled back with a tortoise-shell clip, wearing a pin-striped skirt and a conservative white blouse.

Ali was beautiful no matter what she wore. Any man with eyes in his head was bound to notice.

And Joe wanted her.

The lust he felt startled him. He wasn't going to make it through the day without touching her. He glanced around his office, cursing the modern decor and glass walls—so much for privacy. The decor had never bothered him before now. Would it be too obvious to lower all the shades in his office and call Ali in?

Hell, why should he care? He was the boss. But he had Ali's reputation to worry about.

He pressed his intercom button. "Hi," he said.

"Hi, Joe." Ali glanced at him from her desk and gave a little wave with her fingers. She was only fifteen feet away in her office, but the distance seemed insurmountable. Employees came in and out of her office almost constantly. Again, he damned the glass walls that allowed them no privacy.

"What are you doing for lunch?"

"I wasn't going to take lunch. I'm swamped with—"

"You're taking a lunch, Ali," Joe rasped.

"I am?"

"Yes, you have to take a lunch break. It's the law, and you wouldn't want me to get in trouble for overworking my employees, would you?"

Before she could answer the rhetorical question, he continued. "Have lunch with me today."

"Yes," she breathed into the intercom softly. "I'd like that."

"Meet me in a half hour."

"Where?"

"At Alberto's."

And a short while later, Joe sat across from Ali in a circular corner booth in the Tuscany-style restaurant the Carlino family had half ownership in. It was just the place for two people who wanted a quiet, candlelit lunch.

"This is nice," Ali said, glancing at the stone fountain that obscured them from view from a good part of the restaurant.

Joe watched her intently as she took a look around. When she finally gazed into his eyes, Joe reached for her hand. "I'm going crazy not touching you." He stroked her fingers, rubbing his thumb over them. "Come closer."

Ali scooted closer to him, and Joe's groin tightened. He leaned over to give her a little kiss, but the minute their lips brushed, his heart rate accelerated, and one chaste kiss wasn't enough.

He took her into his arms and dragged her up against him, driving his tongue into her mouth, taking her in a long, drawn out kiss. He reached down to caress her leg, his hand inching up the hem of her skirt, feeling the soft flesh that had driven him wild over the weekend. He moved his hand farther up her thigh, grazing her skin and inching closer to indecency.

Ali pulled back. "Joe." She glanced around. The waiter was heading their way.

"Hell, I usually don't act like a hormone-crazed teenager, Ali." Joe straightened in his seat and lowered his voice. "I told you yesterday that it'd be hard to keep my hands off you."

The waiter approached their table with menus and offered up the day's specials. "Or anything else, you'd like, Mr. Carlino."

"Thank you, Henry. Give us a few minutes to decide."

"Of course. Would you care for a drink?" he asked Ali first.

"A soda for me, please."

Joe needed something stronger. "Scotch on the rocks."

The waiter left, and Ali peered at him, her eyes soft. "You don't usually drink this early in the afternoon."

"There's a lot of things I don't usually do in the afternoon, like grope my—"

"Your?" Ali appeared curious.

"I was going to say, grope my assistant. But you're more than that to me, Ali. I think the weekend proved that."

Ali put her head down. She sighed deeply and hesitated before lifting up to look at him. "I feel the same way, Joe, but there's something I should tell you about my past."

Joe waited, wondering if she'd tell him about her childhood and what it was like for her having so many stepfathers to contend with and having a mother who bounced in and out of relationships. He wanted Ali to explain to him her mother's motives. He hoped the seeds of doubt that Sheila had planted would be washed away with her explanation.

"I was involved with a man once, at work. He hired me under false pretenses. I thought he'd been sincere, but it turned out he wanted a sexual relationship with me. When I wouldn't comply, he made my life very difficult."

"You're not comparing me to him?" Joe blurted.

"No, of course not. But I'm trying to give you an understanding of why I'm cautious. When I told you I don't do one-night stands, I meant it."

Surprised, Joe frowned. It wasn't what he'd expected to hear. Maybe that's why he'd seen changes in Ali. Had she been scarred emotionally from that incident? Ali took pride in her efficiency and competence in the workplace. He couldn't imagine how much that episode in her life might have hurt her. He had to reassure her that he really wasn't an unscrupulous boss out for a brief fling.

"That's not what this is, Ali. I care about you."

His admission made her smile. He should have made that clearer over the weekend. Maybe that's why he'd sensed her holding back. As good as the sex was between them, Joe knew Ali had more to give.

"I care about you, too, Joe."

"I'm not going to pretend I don't want you every minute

of the day. I'm having a hard time staying focused on work with you just a few feet away."

Ali's lips curled up in a sensual smile. "I know the feeling, Joe."

"Invite me over tonight, and I'll be knocking at your door right after work. Hell, I'll even spring for dinner."

Ali's eyes softened, and his hunger for her grew even more powerful. "You're invited."

Joe nodded, imagining mismatched furniture, soft yellow hues and the scent of lavender drifting by as he made love to her in her bedroom.

That's if they'd even make it that far.

Ten

Anticipation coursed through Ali's body the rest of the day. She hadn't been able to concentrate because she was too focused on the idea of Joe coming over after work. She'd lost her focus countless times during the day, going even as far as forgetting who she'd called three seconds after dialing the phone number. She'd stumbled with her greeting until her mind cleared and she finally remembered. After that first episode, Ali decided it wise to jot down the name of the client she'd called and keep it in front of her before she'd made a fool of herself again.

She lived in a haze of desire and tried to avoid making eye contact with Joe in his office for fear of melting into a puddle of lust. At certain times of the day, she knew he watched her, but she held firm and didn't return his gaze. The clock ticked off the minutes at a snail's pace, and she thought the day would never end.

Finally at six o'clock, Ali straightened some papers on

her desk, filed away the rest then grabbed her purse and stood up. She finally braved a glance in Joe's direction. Thankfully, he had his back toward her as he spoke on the phone.

Ali got in her car and drove home, her nerves raw with tension. Once she entered her home, she leaned against the door and breathed in deeply. Joe would be here soon and Ali would have to hold back her innermost desires. She'd have to be Fake Ali again, the submissive girl with no personality and no sense of style. Her reverse makeover had backfired. The guilt she felt deceiving Joe, the man of her dreams, continued to plague her. He was too good a man to dupe this way. "Oh, Ali, what have you gotten yourself into?"

Ali walked to the kitchen and opened the refrigerator. She pulled out a bottle of water and sipped as she contemplated her situation. The only person who would understand all of this was Rena. She'd have to talk to her again about Joe and how much she hated what she was doing to him.

To both of them.

Rena would help. She'd been the voice of reason and a good friend. Thankfully, Ali could turn to her, and she vowed if things didn't get better by the end of the week, she'd have to ask Rena for more advice.

Not three minutes later, Ali heard a knock at her door and her heart skipped a beat. She walked to the front door, took a deep breath and opened it.

Joe glanced over her body in a quick scan. "Good," he said in a rasp, his brows raised, his expression like a wild animal about to devour his prey. "You didn't change out of your clothes."

"I, what?"

He stepped inside, sweeping her into his arms. Kicking the door shut behind him, Clark Kent turned into Superman.

"I've been fantasizing about stripping you out of these clothes all day."

"Oh, Joe." Ali wrapped her arms around him.

Joe nibbled on her throat, then positioned her against the door, grinding his hips to hers.

"You do this to me, Ali."

The strength of his arousal pressed against her.

"I barely made it here without embarrassing myself." He cupped her head and kissed her hastily on the lips, his hands reaching for the buttons of her blouse. "I need to touch you."

Ali helped. As they fumbled with buttons, Joe nearly ripped her blouse in two. He pushed the material off her shoulders. Then he touched her skin, his hands covering her breasts, his lips crushing her mouth. "You're amazing, sweetheart," he groaned.

Ali's joy mounted. Joe wanted her, and she felt his intense need with his every touch. Her body welcomed his frenzied caresses and openmouthed heady kisses.

Ali stood pressed against her door, inviting his assault with little moans and cries of need. She wanted to strip him of his clothes the way he did her. She wanted to push him down to the ground and play out her every fantasy. "I need you, Joe."

"I know, sweet Ali. I know."

His kisses stole her breath, and his fiery need became hers.

He unfastened her bra, and her breasts sprang free of their constraints. A guttural sound escaped his throat, the sound primal and urgent. He cupped her breast with one hand and stroked her with his tongue—his hot breath on her creating spasms of heat inside her body. Ali's pleasure escalated.

She grew tight and wanton within seconds.

Joe sensed her need. He unzipped her pants and lowered them down. She stood before him naked but for a tiny black thong, shimmering with tiny rhinestones that spelled out, All Yours—the one part of Real Ali that was still intact. Her act of rebellion, she thought.

"Sexy," Joe nearly growled.

"I wore them for you."

A gleam sparked in his hungry eyes. "Hell, Ali. I'm going to imagine you in these every time I see you behind your desk."

"You could take them off."

"Oh, don't worry. They're coming off." Then Joe picked her up in his arms. "Later."

She threw her arms around his neck and held on. Joe strode down the hall, kissing her as he moved. She gestured to her bedroom. "I remember," he said. "I've been dying to see the inside of this room."

"Really?"

"Yeah, really."

Joe pulled her quilt back and settled her onto the sheets. She gazed up at him and waited. He looked at her, his eyes intense and gleaming with dark, hot desire. "How'd I get so lucky?"

Joe unbuttoned his shirt, and Ali watched with keen interest. His bronzed chest came into view, and Ali's throat went cotton dry. She'd never tire of seeing him this way.

Next, he kicked off his shoes, removed his socks and finally released himself from the pants that held his straining erection.

He stood naked before her, and Ali's blood pressure skyrocketed. Everything below her navel throbbed with desire. Her nipples peaked to rosy buds.

Joe noticed. He smiled at her in a way that had her moist

between the legs. That's all it took. One hot look from Joe and Ali was toast.

He reached into his pants pocket and tossed a half dozen condoms on her nightstand.

Ali looked at them with a gasp. "Really?"

"We might need to take the day off tomorrow."

Ali shook her head and giggled. She loved Joe more and more each day.

She wanted to gesture to him to come take her. She wanted to tell him six times might not be enough, but Ali only laid there, watching him, his naked form so enticing, so beautiful that she could easily reach out and touch him, bring him as much pleasure as he brought her.

Should she do it? Real Ali would have jumped his bones ten minutes ago. Ali sensed that's what he waited for. Joe wanted more from her. But Ali's passion was so intense that if she ever unleashed it, Joe wouldn't know what hit him.

The question was taken from her when Joe climbed into the bed beside her and took her into his arms. His kisses shut down her mind completely, and she fell into his embrace, allowing him to lead her to oblivion.

Ali woke in the wee hours of the morning with Joe beside her. They'd made love during the night, not quite the half-dozen times they'd set out for but two rather long incredible and satisfying times that would stay etched in Ali's memory forever.

She glanced at her digital alarm clock. It was four in the morning, and they'd be rising soon. She hadn't expected Joe to stay the night, but it warmed her heart that he did. After their last bout of lovemaking, Joe had taken her into his arms, laying her head on his chest and almost instantly fallen asleep.

He stirred restlessly next to her, and she froze, not wanting to wake him. "It's okay, sweetheart. I'm awake."

Ali lifted up from his chest to peer into his eyes. "It's early."

"How early?"

"Four o'clock."

"I should leave before nosy neighbors see me sneaking out of here."

"I don't care what my neighbors think."

Joe chuckled. "No, neither do I. Just thinking about you." He kissed her forehead and brushed loose strands of hair from her face. "I'm always thinking about you."

"That's nice to know."

"Let's take the day off. Play hooky or *do something else*." He caressed her breasts and wiggled his eyebrows, villain style.

Ali giggled then flopped her head back against her pillow and stared at the ceiling. "I wish we could, but you can't do that."

"Why not?"

"I've scheduled two meetings for you today. It would be rude to cancel at the last minute."

"What time?"

"One is at eleven and one is at three in the afternoon."

Joe bent over and kissed her soundly. "That's seven hours from now."

Ali wrapped her arms around his neck. "Yes, that's true."

"We could accomplish a lot in seven hours."

Ali stroked his handsome face. "Especially since you're so thorough."

He did the same. "And you're so efficient."

Joe slid his hands over her, gently, sweetly until he'd caressed every inch of her. "I love touching you."

"I love you touching me." But Ali loved more about Joe than that, and she prayed that Joe would return that love someday to the woman she really was.

At ten that morning, Joe was head deep in work at the office. He'd gotten in around nine, and Ali had gone into work a half hour before him. She'd insisted she had work to do, so he'd gone home after they'd made love once more to take a shower and dress. Sometimes he cursed his practical mind. Both he and Ali realized they had obligations at the office that couldn't be ignored.

So much for playing hooky all day.

Sometimes Joe wished he could be a free spirit, acting on a whim like his brother Nick. His younger sibling had no trouble shirking his responsibilities if a good time was to be had.

Yet, Joe wasn't complaining. He glanced at Ali, her head down, going over some papers at her desk. She looked up, and their eyes met. The soft look on her face gave him pause. Something powerful was happening between them. It was more than lust, and Joe told himself to slow down.

There were things about Ali that he didn't understand. He wanted her to talk about her childhood, have her explain about her mother and also explain how suddenly, her entire demeanor had changed, almost overnight. Ali had gone from flashy and vivacious to conservative and subdued in the span of a few heartbeats it seemed.

For all he knew, it was another of Ali's fashion statements. What Joe didn't know about women could fill volumes, so he didn't dwell on it. But he knew one thing: He and Ali were good together—so good that he got a hard-on just looking at her sometimes.

Joe scratched his neck and chuckled. "Get down to

business," he said to himself. "You've got a meeting in less than an hour."

He finished up a call with a client and then his cell phone rang. He took a quick look at the screen and winced. He really didn't want to have this conversation.

"Hey," he said to Tony.

"Hey, yourself. How've you been?"

"I've got no complaints."

"No? Well, I've had a few. Seems the guy I sent in my place to the Grapegrowers Convention was a no-show. You missed a lot of networking, bro. I've been getting calls for two days asking what happened."

"You know that's not my thing."

"But you went, right?"

"Yeah, I showed up."

"So what happened?"

Joe hesitated, refusing to answer.

"Ah, *Ali* happened."

Joe wasn't a kiss-and-tell kind of guy. He kept his mouth shut.

Tony didn't give him the same courtesy. "At least admit Rena and I were right about the two of you. You couldn't go away with her without playing musical beds."

"Isn't that exactly what you and Rena wanted? And listen, Tony, before you go getting ideas, it was just one weekend."

"Yeah, and the moon is made of marshmallows."

"What?" Joe furrowed his brows.

"You care about Ali. Just admit it."

"Of course I care about her. I'm not...Nick."

Tony laughed. "No, you're a far cry from our baby brother. Don't worry. I won't repeat what you said about him. But Ali's a nice girl, and you, Joe, have been alone way too long."

"Leave the matchmaking to someone who knows what they're doing, bro."

Joe didn't need any more encouragement when it came to Ali. He was having enough trouble sorting out his feelings for her. He'd been gun-shy for so long that he wasn't ready to open up his heart again. And there was always the fact that if it didn't work out between them, that he'd lose the best damn personal assistant on the planet.

All of that aside, Joe liked the status quo at the moment. Sex after work hours had its advantages. Joe glanced at his watch. He had a day full of meetings and work to catch up on. Evening seemed a long time away.

Joe took a look at Ali again, never tiring of seeing her. She was laughing at something Randy Simmons said, and then the sales manager touched her arm. An act of friendship he was sure, but Joe immediately turned away from them. A jolting pang of jealousy ripped through him. He squeezed his eyes shut and counted to three. He had it bad if he couldn't stand to see another man casually touch Ali.

"Joe, you there?"

"I'm here. I'm busy, Tony. I'd better get back to it."

"Okay, fine. And listen, don't worry about blowing off the convention. You're the numbers man. You would know whether we're in good shape or not."

"Trust me, Carlino Wines is doing just fine."

"Great then. Say hello to Ali for me. Oh, and be sure not to work her too hard."

Where did that come from? "I…don't."

"Good, and remember women need at least a few hours of sleep at night."

Joe hit the button on his iPhone to the sound of Tony's deep chuckle.

* * *

At home on Friday night, Ali looked at herself in the mirror, and that same sense of self-loathing plagued her. Wearing no makeup but a little lip gloss and a few swipes of mascara, dressed in a tan pin-striped pantsuit with her wild auburn hair confined in one long braid down her back, Ali frowned. She took her glasses off and laid them down on the dressing table. "Who are you, Ali Pendrake?"

But Ali knew the image in the mirror wasn't her. She hated the clothes she wore, and that hadn't changed. She'd hoped that slowly she'd morph into a woman who enjoyed dressing down, who enjoyed the conservative look of a businesswoman.

"You," she said pointing to the mirror, "are not *me*."

It wasn't only the clothes that bothered her. She'd faked her subdued personality, biting her tongue each time a sassy comment came to mind. She couldn't say what she wanted. She couldn't do what she wanted. So many times she wanted to express her feelings to Joe. She wanted to disagree with him about politics and religion and shout at him that rock music wasn't just a bunch of garbage.

She wanted to be herself.

She loved Joe Carlino with all of her heart, but she wasn't being fair to him or to herself with this charade. She was like a little kid who'd caught a big fish and then didn't know what to do with it.

Joe was her big fish. He was the love of her life. But he hadn't been even remotely attracted to the Real Ali Pendrake. One year's worth of hoping had proven that. So why on earth hadn't she let things be?

Now, it was too late. She was in love too deeply to get out without horrid injury. She didn't know if she was brave enough to tell him the truth.

"Who are you?" she asked again to the reflection in the mirror.

The week had been magical on the Joe front. She'd see him at the office during the day, and the hunger in his eyes reassured her that she couldn't let him go. He'd catch her in a private moment at work and steal a quick kiss, saying it was his sustenance until they'd met at night.

He'd come over with dinner each evening after work, but they never managed to eat their meal until the midnight hour, too consumed with each other to feel any other sort of hunger but the sexual kind.

Ali was in heaven while he was with her.

But she was in her own private hell when they were apart.

Tonight, she actually begged off with Joe. She needed an escape from Fake Ali for one night. She needed to be herself.

Joe had frowned when she told him she had a cooking lesson with Royce that would go late into the evening. She could see it was on the tip of his tongue to offer to come over after her lesson, but he'd held back. Maybe he'd hoped she would be the one to do the inviting, or maybe, he realized they needed a short break from each other. They'd been together every day and night for one entire week.

Ali kicked off her brown pumps, slipped out of her pantsuit and unbraided her hair. She ran her hands through the strands, and as her hair loosened from their bonds, so had Ali. She felt free, alive. Herself.

She turned on the radio, and a U-2 song blasted out. Ali danced her way to the shower, stepped inside and sang along with the radio, washing her hair, soaping her body and rinsing off as she moved with the music.

She toweled off, fingered through her hair, allowing it to dry naturally for the time being. Later, she'd take a round brush to it and use the blow-dryer to add more wispy curls.

Ali walked to her closet and spread the hangers wide, ignoring her Fake Ali clothes. She picked out a pair of black jeans and nodded. "I've missed you," she said, stroking the material as she would a long, lost love.

Next she searched for just the right blouse. She found a black silk that had gold tones of op art emblazoned on the front, the neck high on her throat, but the back dipping low with crisscrossing straps. She grabbed her leather boots from the floor of her closet and sighed. "I've missed you, too."

Ali opened her jewelry box and went right to a pair of thin, gold hoop earrings. Without pause, she set them onto her earlobes and stepped back from her dresser to admire them. "Nice."

She put her face on—a little blush on her cheeks, eyeliner and shadow to enhance the jade color of her eyes—and then lined her lips with cherry-red lipstick. She finished off her hair with the blow-dryer, then dressed in the clothes she'd picked out and stepped into her foyer where she could view herself in the full-length mirror. She liked what she saw.

The knock came at her door at precisely eight o'clock, and Ali was ready for Royce.

"Wow," he said, glancing at her with keen interest. He had a nice way about him, and some women might think him incredibly handsome in that blond, surfer looking kind of way. He held a grocery bag full of items for the lesson.

"Come in," she said, allowing him entrance. "What are we making tonight?"

"Well, I uh," Royce didn't take his eyes off her. "You look dynamite, Ali. Are you expecting someone else, later?"

Ali laughed. “No way. I’m up for our cookout.”

“Really, because you look too gorgeous to stay home and make dinner. If I had half a brain, I’d offer to take you dancing. I have a friend who plays guitar in a band, and he’s got a gig tonight in Yountville.”

Ali opened her eyes wide, tempted to take Royce up on it. “Gosh, I haven’t been to a concert since I left New York.”

Royce narrowed his eyes. “Are you saying you want to go?”

Ali took the grocery bag out of his arms and marched to the kitchen. “How about we make dinner first, and if there’s time, I’d love to go.”

Royce followed her into the kitchen. “Sounds good to me.” Then Royce cast a thoughtful look her way. “Hey, Ali, why’d you call me out of the blue?”

She turned away from the groceries she’d been removing from the bag and smiled. “We’re friends, aren’t we?”

“Yeah, but you’ve been busy lately.”

“I know I have. The truth is I missed having a friend to talk to.”

“You can’t talk to your, uh, boyfriend?”

Ali only smiled. She couldn’t give Royce a good explanation without spilling her whole sordid deception.

“Is he out of town?”

“No! I wouldn’t do that to you, Royce. The fact is, he wanted to come over tonight, but I realized I’ve been neglecting my friends. Besides,” she said, poking him gently in the shoulder, “you need to teach me how to make—” She frowned. She didn’t know what they’d be making tonight.

“Beef tenderloin with wild mushroom sauce.”

“My mouth is watering already! So go on, teach away.”

Royce laughed and gazed at her mouth in a dangerous way. She'd told him countless times they were friends and hoped he wasn't reading more into this evening than that. He'd never really made a pass at her, and she trusted her instincts.

The one really good thing about being with Royce was that he liked her for herself. And she could simply *be,* when she was with him.

Royce immediately began barking commands, teaching her about different cuts of meat and how to look for marbling in the pieces she'd find at the market. He showed her how to prepare it and then went on to teach her how to make the wild mushroom sauce. He was actually a very good instructor, and Ali could tell how passionate he was about cooking.

By nine o'clock the meal was ready and they sat down to eat. Ali felt a measure of guilt when she thought about Joe. What was he doing now? She missed him terribly, but at the same time, she felt good about herself tonight. Like she'd reconnected to Real Ali. So much so, that after they ate the savory meal, she agreed to go dancing with Royce.

"Just for a little while," she said on their way to Yountville. "I've had a busy week, and I'm a little tired," she said.

Royce agreed. "No problem, Ali. We'll have a drink and dance a little. I've been meaning to hear Charley's new band. He'll be glad I showed up. Consider this a favor for the cooking lesson."

Ali relaxed more, glad that Royce didn't view this as any sort of date.

When Royce pulled into the back parking lot of the small club, music blared out from the open doors. He parked the car, and they walked around to the front of the building.

They entered Rock and a Hard Place, and immediately Ali loved the look of the small venue. It wasn't a trendy New York club but a more rustic place with sawdust on the floor and a long wall-to-wall dark oak bar.

"They're on now," Royce said, pushing through a small crowd to bring her closer to the stage. He pointed to a band member with longish hair and ripped jeans. "That's Charley on the guitar."

Royce shot him a quick wave, and Charley nodded.

"What's the name of their band?" she asked.

"Guts and Glory."

Ali laughed and Royce joined in. "I know. Not exactly Bon Jovi or Queen, but they sound good."

"They do," Ali said, clapping her hands and tapping her feet to the music.

Royce leaned over to speak into her ear. "Want a drink?"

Ali had to raise her voice over the band to answer. "Sure. Whatever you're drinking is fine."

A few minutes later, Royce returned with two mojitos. He handed her one, and she took a sip. "It's good. Thanks!"

Royce stood beside her until they'd both finished their drinks. "Want another?" he asked. "Or are you ready to dance?"

"Dance."

Royce took her hand and led her onto the small, crowded dance floor. The band played all fast tunes, and Ali let loose, dancing in sync with the beat, despite bumping into other couples for lack of space. She laughed with Royce over the loud music, tossed her hair to and fro and shimmied with the best of them. After five back-to-back dances, Royce came close enough to ask if she wanted another drink.

Ali debated and finally nodded. "One more. But I'll

get them for us." She felt better about paying her own way. Royce frowned but relented, and she stood at the bar with sweat dripping from her brow. She took a napkin and quickly wiped it away.

She was enjoying herself and burning calories, what more could a girl ask?

The band took a break, and as she waited at the bar for their drinks, she saw Royce speaking with his friend Charley by the stage.

A man sidled up next to her, and Ali turned, coming face-to-face with Nick Carlino.

"You're a great dancer, Ali."

"Nick, hi." Ali kept the panic from her voice. She could only imagine what Nick was thinking. Judging by his compliment, he must have been watching her dance with Royce. "Thanks. I love it."

Nick smiled. "Do you come here often?"

He made his point with the cliché pickup line, and Ali also knew that he was darn curious about her being here with Royce.

"No, I've never actually been here before." Ali brushed her unruly hair from her face, a gesture Nick didn't miss. "My neighbor Royce invited me to see his friend play. He's in the band." She pointed, but Nick didn't bother looking.

"What are you doing here?" she asked.

"I'm on a date."

"Oh, really?" Ali scanned the room but couldn't find the woman he was with.

"She's in the back, taking care of business, I presume. There was a problem with one of her employees."

Puzzled, Ali asked. "What kind of business?"

Nick grinned. "She owns the place."

Ali shook her head and smiled back at him. "I should have known."

"I like you, Ali. In fact, if Joe wasn't in the picture—"

"But Joe's very much in the picture," she finished for him.

"Doesn't look like it tonight."

"We don't spend all our nights together," Ali said in her own defense. Although since their trip to San Francisco, they had been inseparable. "And Royce is a good friend. That's all."

"Hey, I'm not accusing you of anything. I have my eye on your *friend,* though, just in case. If he'd so much as made an improper gesture toward you, I'd have decked him."

"Would you?" Ali asked, not sure Nick was telling the truth. He was a charmer with a killer smile and a man used to getting his own way, yet she didn't figure him as the brute type.

"For Joe. Yeah, I would." Nick braced his arm against the bar and looked her dead in the eyes. "Are you going to tell him about tonight?"

Ali blinked. "I suppose. It's no big deal."

"Just be sure that you do. And don't mention you saw me here."

"Why not?"

"Because then he'd be pissed at me for not telling him I saw you." Nick winked. "He's a good guy, Ali. Don't trample him. He's been there and done that once already."

"I wouldn't hurt Joe for the world."

"Good. Just keep it that way."

Ali sipped the mojito the bartender put in front of her. "You Carlinos stick together, don't you?"

"Like glue."

Ali wished she had someone who watched her back,

the way Nick just had for his brother. Most times she was on the giving end with friends and family. Both her father and mother had sought her out when they needed help, and Ali was glad to give it. But she'd never asked for the same in return. She'd grown up independent of others out of necessity. Her mother's frivolous lifestyle hadn't allowed for her to develop close ties.

It was at this moment that Ali realized that she harbored resentment toward both her parents—maybe a childish notion, but she'd wished they watched her back and put her first, just once.

Nick picked up two drinks the bartender sent his way. "Gotta go find my date." He began to leave, then stopped and turned around, his gaze flowing over her from top to bottom, assessing her hair, her face, her breasts and all the way down to her black leather boots. "I like the look, Ali. I think Joe would, too."

Heat crawled up her neck, and she was darn glad that Nick had taken off before he saw how much his comment affected her. It was almost as if Nick had figured her out.

What if he had? What if he knew the truth? He'd seen her cut loose, dancing like a maniac, drinking and laughing with another man. Did he know she was a fraud? She feared that he did and that would spell disaster.

Ali knew her deception had to end. She had to call it quits and confess to Joe what she'd done. She had to hope he felt enough for her, to give his forgiveness. If she'd injured him in anyway, she'd never forgive herself.

Ali was on unsure footing here. She could think of a dozen worst-case scenarios, and each of them made her cringe with regret and anguish. But one thought preyed on her sense of optimism and gave her hope.

Maybe Joe would laugh it off and tell her he loved her no matter what.

Somehow, she didn't see that happening.

A tremble coursed through her body, a quick shiver of impending doom. Ali couldn't shake off the feeling that things were about to go from bad to worse.

When Royce returned, she handed him his drink. "Please drink it fast," she said to him, urgently. "I need to go home."

Eleven

Ali tossed and turned that night, unable to sleep. She missed having Joe beside her, listening to the sound of his breathing and waking next to him in the morning. She missed his kisses and the steady way he held her.

She finally managed to get a few hours of sleep, and when sunlight beamed its way into her bedroom, Ali glanced at the clock. It was after six, and Joe would be taking his morning swim soon.

Ali rose slowly, reminded of her restlessness from last night by a headache that throbbed in her skull. She rubbed her temples and padded to the kitchen to set coffee brewing. Her motions were by rote, one step in front of the other, and gradually, after she drank a cup of coffee and ate a piece of buttered toast, the ache in her head subsided.

"Okay, Ali. Be brave. Pick up the phone and call Joe."

Ali waited ten more minutes, reciting in her head what she'd planned to tell him. Once she was sure he was out of the pool and dried off, according to his precise timetable, Ali picked up the phone.

She was greeted with a cheerful voice. "Good morning, sweetheart."

"Joe," she said with a sigh. Just the sound of his deep, sexy voice did things to her. "Hello."

"How was your cooking lesson?"

"It went well. I think I could duplicate the dish for you one night."

"I'd like that."

"I, uh, missed you last night."

"Same here, honey."

"What did you do?" *Ali, quit stalling. Tell him about last night and then ask to speak with him in person.*

"Tony and Rena stopped by. They entertained me for most of the night."

"That's nice."

"It was, actually."

"How is Rena feeling these days?"

"She looked great, healthy. She's a lot of fun. She even makes Tony tolerable."

Ali didn't respond to his little jibe. Instead, she began her explanation. "Joe, last night after Royce's lesson, he asked me to do him a favor."

"What kind of favor?"

"Just to go with him to a club. I think it's called Rock and a Hard Place, if you can believe that. He had a friend playing in the band and so I went with him, and we listened to the band and had a few drinks."

"Did you enjoy it?"

Ali decided the truth was her best option. If she was going to come clean with Joe, now was the best time to start. "The band was pretty good, actually. Great dance music. Yes, it was fun."

"You danced?"

"I did, Joe."

She heard Joe take a long, deep pull of air. Then silence ensued for what seemed like an eon. "What are you doing right now?"

"Now? I just finished breakfast. I'm not even dre—"

"Don't go anywhere. I'll be over in less than an hour."

Joe hung up the phone before Ali could respond. "That went well," she said, her body shaking. She couldn't tell if Joe was furious or not. She had no idea what he was thinking. Joe didn't wear his heart on his sleeve. He was steady and even and practical minded most of the time.

Ali hopped in the shower and dressed, with her eyes on the clock. If Joe said he'd be over in less than an hour, she knew he wouldn't be late. She had her clothes all picked out for today. It was Saturday, and she'd thought she'd put on her tight stone-washed jeans and something wild and colorful. But Ali changed her mind at the last minute. She donned a brown knit blouse and beige slacks and then put her curly hair back into a tight ponytail. "You're a chicken, Ali Pendrake," she said, sliding her eyeglasses on.

She paced the room and finally settled down with a *People* magazine. She sat on the edge of her sofa and flipped through the pages until she came upon an article that held her moderate interest. Attempting to concentrate on a blurb about upcoming summer blockbuster movies, the doorbell rang. Ali jumped off her perch and tossed the magazine aside. Her nerves jangling, she strode to the front door.

With one hand on the doorknob, Ali took a deep breath, closed her eyes and said a little prayer. Then she opened the door slowly, afraid of what she might find on the other side.

Joe stood on her doorstep, wearing a grim expression,

yet holding a big bouquet of the most gorgeous white lilies Ali had ever seen. Her mouth gaped open in surprise. Joe strode over her threshold, and after she closed the door, she turned to him in question. Without a second's notice, he pressed his mouth to hers in a long leisurely I-missed-you kind of kiss that would have knocked her socks off had she been wearing any. He backed away after that awesome kiss and handed her the flowers.

"For you, sweetheart."

Tears welled in her eyes. She didn't understand any of this, but she was grateful she'd been given a slight reprieve. "Thank you. They're beautiful. But what's the occasion?"

"No occasion." Joe took her hand in his. "I'm not the most romantic soul, Ali," he confessed, using his other hand to move his eyeglasses up his nose. "But I really care about you, and I don't want to take advantage of our situation. We haven't dated at all. Hell, I've barely fed you dinner this week, much less taken you out."

"We've had other things to do," Ali said aloud.

"Yeah, we have. But you deserve more."

"Joe, if this is about last night, it was completely innocent. Really, I have no interest in Royce. You have to know that."

"I know it, or I'd be beating down his door right now."

Apparently, Nick wasn't the only macho Carlino. Ali almost smiled at the image of Superman Joe, taking on Royce, the surfer dude.

"But it was a wake-up call for me, Ali. I've only been in this partway. It's my fault, and I want to make it up to you."

"It's not your fault. There is no fault." Ali almost couldn't bear to hear him out. *She* was the one at fault, not Joe. Guilt ate at her, weakening her knees. She hugged the lilies to her chest.

"Ali, I've got a vacation coming up in a month. I wasn't going to take it, but I've changed my mind. I want you to come with me to our villa in the Bahamas. I think you'd love it."

Staggered by his offer, and the implications that he wanted to share his vacation with her, Ali needed to sit down. She plopped on the sofa as myriad emotions caught her by surprise. Joy and love burst forth, but then self-loathing and guilt reared its ugly head, destroying her good mood. "Joe, that's so…um, I don't have the words."

"How about yes? That's the word I want to hear."

She couldn't refuse Joe anything, much less a chance to be with him at a tropical paradise. "Yes."

Joe smiled then reached for her, crushing the flowers she held between them, and kissed her again. "Good. I'll make the arrangements. We'll take a week. I'll show you a good time, Ali."

"Joe, you always do."

He grinned and stroked her cheek. "Do you have plans tomorrow?"

She thought for a second, then shook her head. "No."

"Great. I've rescheduled our bike tour. That was our deal, and I'm following through. You still want to see Napa?"

She'd follow him anywhere. "Yes, I look forward to it."

"Great, well, I've got to get busy. How about dinner tonight?"

Ali smiled at him while a little voice in her head nagged that her inner chicken was hiding in the hen house. "I'd love it."

He gave her a quick nod and looked deep into her eyes.

"This time, I'm taking you to the nicest restaurant in Napa."

"But Joe, you don't—"

Joe put a finger to her lips. "Shh, Ali." He bent his head and brushed a soft kiss to her mouth. "I'll be dusting off my tux, so be ready."

Ali leaned heavily on the door as soon as Joe left. Her heart in her throat, she felt as though she'd run a marathon without benefit of water. Everything went limp, including the smile she'd shown Joe.

Tears threatened to spill down her face, but she managed to hold her emotions in check and march over to her kitchen phone. She should have done this much sooner.

"Hi, Rena," she said softly into the phone. "It's Ali, and I need your help."

"It's a good thing I insisted you come over this morning, hon. I could hear by the sound of your voice earlier that you were upset." Rena set a cup of tea in front of Ali on a charming round table for two in the Purple Fields gift shop. "I hated to bother you," Ali said quietly.

"No bother. As you can see, we're not busy this time of day. We have the whole place to ourselves."

"Thanks. But with the baby coming soon and the construction on your house, I didn't want to give you added drama."

Rena chuckled and gestured wide with her arms. "Give me drama. *Please,* give me drama. My life is so sedate these days that I'm ready to pull my hair out. Tony takes care of the business mostly, and I'm done with picking floor samples and paint colors." She patted her rotund belly. "Tony tells me to relax now because when the baby comes, I'll be superbusy, but relaxing isn't easy. I've never been one to sit and let the world go by."

"Right now that sounds good to me," Ali said.

"So, what's going on? I presume there are problems with Joe?"

"Yes, but it's probably not what you're thinking." Ali paused to sigh deeply before sharing with Rena her innermost feelings. "I love him very much. I do, and he's been wonderful to me. We have a great time together. That's why I'm so afraid to tell him the truth. I almost did this morning. I almost told him that I've been deceiving him and that the woman he asked to go away with him to the Bahamas is a fake. He thinks I'm someone I'm not. But I chickened out when he brought flowers and asked me to take a vacation with him. How could I refuse that? It's a dream come true."

"Oh, Ali. Is it really that bad?"

"Yeah, it is." A self-deprecating laugh followed. "Look at me? Look at what I'm wearing." Ali pulled at her preppy-looking cotton blouse. "This isn't me. But worse than the clothes, I'm not being true to myself, and I've hit a wall. I can't stand it anymore. I've bitten my tongue so many times around Joe that it's a wonder I can speak at all. I want Joe but not at the expense of fooling him the rest of his life."

Rena sipped her tea and listened carefully.

"Do you think you and Joe…is it serious?"

"For me, yes. For Joe, I think so. At least I'm hoping so. I know he cares for me." She smiled when she thought about this past week and how hungry they'd been for each other. The overtures Joe made this week had been so endearing and thrilling that she could only assume that their relationship would move ahead.

Yet, she had one more confession to make. "Even in the bedroom I'm holding back," she said bluntly. "I'm not the passive sex partner I've portrayed myself to be." Ali worried that she'd overstepped her bounds sharing that detail, but Rena hadn't even blinked. "Sorry, but I had to tell someone."

"It's okay, Ali. You can share anything with me. I'll keep whatever you tell me confidential."

"I'm such a fraud." Ali stared out the little window she sat beside, looking into flourishing vines in the distance. "And I've been too cowardly to tell him that I'm not the person he thinks I am. I've tried, but I'm afraid of losing him."

Rena took her hand and squeezed. "Ali, if you want my advice, I'll give it to you."

"Please." Ali desperately needed help in sorting this out. "If you have any suggestions, I'm listening."

"Don't tell him."

Ali blinked rapidly a few times. "But that means that I'd have to go on pretending."

"Show him." Rena cast her a reassuring smile.

"Show him?" Puzzled, Ali nibbled on her lower lip and shook her head. "I don't get how."

"Show him who you are. Be yourself, Ali. Dress the way you want. Say what you want, and for goodness' sake, don't hold anything back in the bedroom. If Joe cares enough about you, he'll accept you for you."

Ali saw the logic in that. "It makes sense when you say it, but it still scares me."

"Ali, if Joe can't love you for yourself then do you really want him?"

Ali mulled that over for second or two then nodded in agreement with Rena. "Good point."

"I'm sorry I got you into this, Ali. If I'd known it would have given you so much anguish, I would have never suggested your little makeover in reverse."

"You have nothing to be sorry about. If anything, at least you've given me a chance with Joe."

"I hope so."

Ali gained newfound strength. "I'm going to do it, Rena. I'm saying goodbye to Fake Ali for good. Next time you see me, you might not recognize me." Her mood lightened, and tension released from her body. The cloud she'd been under had lifted. "God, I feel so free, just saying it!" She rose and hugged Rena. "Thank you."

"Let me know how it goes, hon."

"I will. I'm taking a gamble. But that's what I always do. I just hope I snatch the brass ring this time."

"Got a hot date?" Nick sauntered into the living room, just as Joe was pouring himself a drink at the bar.

"Maybe."

"No maybe about it. You don't dress in a monkey suit unless you want to impress the hell out of a woman."

Joe turned to his brother and grinned. "Yeah, I guess you're right." The whiskey slid down his throat easily. He glanced at his watch, wishing the time would go by quickly. He had thirty minutes to kill before picking Ali up.

"I am? You mean, you're admitting it?"

"Yeah, I won't deny it." Joe leaned against the long, polished bar and folded his arms across his middle.

"And you're smiling from ear to ear. Be careful, Joey. You might find yourself—"

"I know all the warnings, Nick. And for once, I don't care. I think Ali is the right woman for me."

Nick walked over to pour himself a drink. He offered Joe another, but he shook his head. "Really? It only took you over a year to figure it out."

"I'm slow on the uptake, but I finish with flying colors," Joe said.

Nick chuckled and took a swallow of whiskey. "I couldn't have said it better myself."

"I said it for you, so you couldn't gloat."

"Oh, don't worry. I'm gloating and a bit envious. Ali's pretty spectacular."

"I agree. She's not like most women."

Nick smirked and shook his head, and Joe didn't know why that look annoyed him so much.

"What?"

"Don't be naive, Joe. One thing I know is women. They all want the same thing—money, power, status and lucky for us, we're in the position to give them that."

"Cynical, Nick."

"Realistic. But hey, I'm glad you're coming out of the cave Sheila trapped you in. I hope it works out for you."

Nick finished his drink, slapped him on the back in a show of real affection and left.

Twenty minutes later, Joe knocked briskly on Ali's front door, anticipating the night ahead. He tucked his hands in his pockets and when she opened the door, Joe's mouth fell open. "Wow."

Ali stood before him, and the first thing he noticed was her auburn hair flowing down her shoulders in a mass of curls. Her hair looked untamed and amazingly free. Glancing from her hair to a face that positively beamed, he peered into jade-green eyes that looked twice their size and weren't hidden behind eyeglasses. Her smile brought his focus to her lips colored to a dark pink hue. Full, lush and so kissable, Joe held his willpower in check, determined to give Ali the romantic night he'd planned.

But as his gaze dipped lower, Joe's intake of breath was loud enough to bring on another smile from Ali. Her sexy black dress clung to her body like a second skin—and how that crisscrossing material kept her beautiful cleavage from spilling out could possibly be the eighth wonder of the world.

Her dress stopped short of her knees. Three-inch black high-heeled sandals supported tanned, gorgeous legs that went on forever.

"You like?" she asked, whirling around in a slow circle.

Joe caught a glimpse of her soft shoulders and lower back and all the skin exposed by her dress before she turned to face him.

"You look beyond beautiful, Ali."

"And you look sexy, Joe. I like the tux." She tugged on his arm and enticed him inside.

"No," he said, stopping short and grabbing her hand. Immediate heat radiated between them. He'd have her out of that dress in two seconds flat if he gave in to what he was feeling.

"No?" Ali asked, her lips forming a pout.

"C'mon, sweetheart. If I come inside, we'll never make dinner. Go get your things. I'll wait for you out here."

Joe stepped outside and waited, telling himself he'd done the right thing. With the way Ali looked tonight, all glittery and beaming, he wouldn't have had a chance if he'd strayed inside her condo with the bedroom only steps away.

Hell, forget the bedroom. He might not have made it that far.

Joe drew in a steady breath, allowing the crisp Napa air to cool his jets. *You promised her a great evening, so stick to the plan, Joe.*

When Ali joined him, holding a small purse and wearing a little black shawl around her shoulders, Joe put his hand to her back and escorted her to the limo.

"I know," he said before she could ask. "I debated, but I conserved water today, recycled cans and planted a vegetable garden."

"With your bare hands?" she asked, looking at him like he could save the world.

"No. The gardener did it, but it was my idea."

Ali laughed lightly, and the sound of her joy made him grin from ear to ear.

"Okay, so you get credit for the idea," she said.

"Is that cheating?"

"Not in my book. It's called clever maneuvering, Joe. To be honest, I'd expect Nick to dream something like that up."

"Hey, at least we'll make up for the limo ride tomorrow when we take our bike ride."

"True," Ali said, and the chauffeur opened the door for them. Ali slipped inside and Joe followed, aware of every movement she made in her dress.

Heat climbed up his neck, and he grew hard instantly.

"What's the matter, Joe?"

"Nothing that can't be fixed in a few hours from now. Just keep to the far side of the seat and don't look at me that way."

"Okay," Ali said with a sweet smile that somehow appeared wickedly sinful.

Joe groaned and kept his focus out the window the entire way to the restaurant.

Joe's blatantly sexy gaze was on Ali as they ate dinner atop a hill in a gorgeous mansion transformed into a top-notch restaurant, called quite simply The Mansion. Ali's mother and one of her right-then husbands had dragged her to many classy country clubs as a child, but no place she'd ever been to could compare to this.

Darkly textured stone walls and romantically lit tables were surrounded by old-world elegance in a tall room with sweeping sheer drapes that opened to the magnificence of the valley below. Crystal chandeliers, plush carpets and waiters dressed in tuxedos made an impressive picture. Soft music played by a five-piece orchestra added to the ambience.

The menu, a leather-bound book of choices, had given her a heart attack as she imagined what each entrée would cost. Joe was a rich man, but this extravagance was totally out of character for him. Yet, he looked good in the surroundings, blending in with the decor and not intimidated at all by the elegance. Thankfully, he'd ordered for both of them and picked a fine wine to go with the meal.

Joe gave her his full attention during dinner, entertaining her with the history of The Mansion and telling stories of his youth, growing up in Napa.

After the meal, Joe stood and reached for her hand. "Dance with me."

Ali rose, and he led her onto the dance floor.

"Is this your first-date way to impress a woman?" she asked as they stepped onto the wooden flooring.

"I don't know." He took her into his arms, bringing her up close. "Am I impressing you?"

"Oh, yeah, Joe. You're impressing the heck out of me."

He chuckled and drew her even closer.

Ali wound her arms around his neck. "You might even get lucky tonight, boss." She nibbled on his throat.

"Ali," Joe warned in a low tone, his sharp inhalation very telling.

"What, Joe?"

"They make a great chocolate soufflé here. I want us to last at least through dessert."

"Then maybe you shouldn't have asked me to dance," she whispered.

"I had to," he said. "In case you hadn't noticed, you turned a lot of heads when you walked in."

How could she have noticed? She only had eyes for Joe. "Oh, so you're staking your claim?"

Joe grinned. "Something like that. And you looked so beautiful in candlelight that I had to touch you."

Ali rested her head on his chest, and he tightened his hold on her. "You're saying all the right things."

"Am I passing the first-date test?"

"With flying colors."

Joe chuckled, and when she peered up at him in question, he simply shook his head, smiling.

"Did I say something funny?"

"Not at all. You just repeated something I'd said to Nick earlier."

Ali let that comment go and didn't question him further. Being held in his arms as the violinist played a sweetly romantic tune was heaven on earth.

They moved slowly, erotically. Ali's hips brushed Joe's, her body flowing into his with intimate little touches—a sort of public foreplay that had her mind whirling.

Joe kissed her forehead, caressed her back and ran his hands through her hair, his body rock hard.

Show him who you are. Rena's advice came through loud and clear, and Ali wouldn't stop now.

"You think we could get the soufflé to go?" she asked urgently in a breathless tone that was true to her nature. "I want to feed it to you myself privately."

Joe stopped dancing and stared at her. He blinked several times and grinned. With a hot gleam in his eyes, he dragged her off the dance floor. "Let's go."

Twelve

They made out in the back of the limo, unable to keep their hands off each other. Ali climbed onto his lap, and Joe's control nearly snapped. He ran his hand underneath her dress and stroked her thigh, skimming the soft flesh. Ali's moan of pleasure had his erection pulsing.

Ali seemed different tonight, but Joe wasn't questioning it. He was as hungry for her as she was for him. They stumbled up to her apartment, Ali tugging at his tie, loosening it. She opened the door, and they fumbled their way in.

When Joe wanted to take her straight to the bedroom, Ali shook her head and led him to the kitchen. "Dessert, remember?"

Joe protested with a groan and wished they hadn't taken the chocolate soufflé to go.

"I promise you that you won't be sorry." She removed

his jacket and then his tie and offered him a seat at her kitchen table.

When he glanced at her puzzled, she gave a little shove. "Sit."

Joe sat.

She came around from the back, her exotic scent invading his senses, and with nimble hands she unbuttoned his shirt. She stroked his chest, running her hands up and down. He loved when she touched him. She rarely took the initiative, which confirmed that something was up with her tonight.

He pulled her down to kiss her, and when he tried to do more, she backed away. "Hold that thought. I'll be right back."

Joe waited just a minute before Ali shut down the lights in the room. She came back with one vanilla scented pillar candle glowing and the chocolate delicacy on a plate with one fork. She set the candle down on the table along with the plate.

Next, Ali stood before him and slipped out of her dress. The material pooled at her feet. She stepped out of it, and Joe looked at the most gorgeous woman he'd ever seen. The strain in his pants was now an ache.

Ali wore a tiny bra that barely contained her ample breasts, the nipples a faint hint through the lacy material. A little black stretch of fabric covered the vee between her legs and enticed him beyond belief. Ali had never undressed before him. She'd never been so bold. "If you're trying to kill me, you're succeeding."

Ali smiled, a sensual curving of her lips. "That comes later, baby. First I'm going to feed you."

Ali straddled his legs and took up the dessert plate. She forked into the chocolate concoction and lifted it to his lips. "Open your mouth, Joe."

Her breasts were at eye level and so beautiful. "My mouth has better things to—"

Ali set the fork into his mouth. The chocolate oozed inside and melted into his mouth.

"How is it?"

Joe glanced at the picture she made straddling him nearly naked. "Amazing."

"Now my turn," Ali said, forking a piece and opening her mouth wide. She inserted the fork in and Joe's throat constricted. She chewed briefly then swallowed, licking her lips. "Delicious."

Then she leaned over to kiss him, and he didn't miss the opportunity to drive his tongue into her mouth. She tasted sweet and sexy, and he took his time with her.

"I think we can do better," she said. She set the fork down and dipped her fingers into the soufflé. She pressed the cake into his mouth then brushed a soft kiss to his lips. He chewed quickly and lifted her messy fingers to his tongue, licking off the chocolate, one finger at a time. The heady maneuver broke him out in a sweat.

"Ali," he groaned. "I can't take much more of this."

She plopped a piece of chocolate cake into her mouth and swallowed. "You have a little on your mouth," she said. She leaned in and swirled her tongue onto his upper lip until he burned with dire need.

Joe's willpower shut down.

He pulled out the chair and grabbed her around the waist. "Wrap your legs around me," he ordered. And once she did, Joe bounded up from the chair, Ali's legs tight around his waist.

He knew his way to the bedroom and made quick work of lowering her down on her bed.

But Ali didn't stay down. She rose up on her knees. "Let me undress you."

Joe surrendered immediately. Ali lowered the sleeves of his shirt and pulled it off. Her hands found his chest again, and her touch made his straining erection throb harder.

She caressed him for a few seconds there before sliding her hands down lower to unfasten his belt. She pulled it free, then brought her tongue to his navel and laved it, moistening his skin thoroughly. Joe kicked off his shoes and slipped his feet out of his socks, waiting. Anticipating. Her next move didn't disappoint. Ali unzipped his pants, lowered them down along with his briefs and then glanced at his manhood. "Impressive," she said with a sexy grin.

Joe didn't need any more encouragement. He was almost at his limit.

Ali cupped him with her hands, and Joe managed to hold on, enjoying every minute of Ali's foreplay. She stroked him gently, her soft hands on his silken flesh. He braced his hands on her shoulders, needing to touch her as she pleasured him. Her hand slid over him in ways that he'd only dreamt about, and he grabbed handfuls of her hair in both hands gently encouraging her to go on. But this was Ali, he kept saying to himself, and he wondered why tonight was different. *She* was different. She didn't hold back in any way. She drove him absolutely wild. The picture she made on the bed was a visual he'd not soon forget.

Then, she took him into her mouth. "Oh, yes," he muttered through gritted teeth. Ali held his hips and worked magic on him with her perfect mouth. Her tongue caressed his shaft and flames erupted. He held her hair tight as she moved on him. Little moans of pleasure erupted from her throat, and Joe's whole body gave in to her, allowing her to have her way. He enjoyed every ounce of her sensual assault, whispering his praise in full surrender.

It wasn't long before he reached his limit. He stopped

Ali, pulled her away and climbed onto the bed, taking her with him. "Hang on to your hat, sweetheart."

He entered her in one fully satisfying deep thrust. She was ready for him, and he could always count on that. He moved quickly, fiercely, his memory of what she'd just done to him, making short work of filling her with his powerful need. They climaxed together, the quick joining just chapter one of a very long night ahead.

Joe dozed after that, with a big smile on his face. He heard Ali rise and the shower go on. He pictured her in there, soaping up, scenting her body with some delicious fragrance, and he thought about joining her. But before those thoughts came to fruition, Ali walked into the room bare naked, wet hair flowing down her back and her face scrubbed clean looking natural and pure. Droplets of water glistened all over her body, her breasts full and ripe, nipples erect. Water clung to the tips, and Joe itched to lick those drops off her.

He lifted from the bed to do just that, but Ali stopped him with a gentle hand. "Lay back, Joe. Tonight I'm the boss."

Joe's eyes went wide. "Sounds good."

"Oh, it *is* good."

Joe imagined the most erotic things a woman and a man could do in a bedroom, and his heart began pumping like an oil rig striking a full-on gusher. And in the next hours, most of those erotic imaginings became staggering and stunning memories.

Joe leaned back with amazed joy as Ali straddled him one more time, riding him up and down, her hair dry now and flowing in wild curls past her shoulders, her beautiful body arching, her breasts tipped toward the ceiling, her face glowing and ready to fracture with the shattering of her next powerful orgasm.

They'd had several through the night, each one different and amazing.

Joe held her, stroked her breasts, flicking the tips, and watched Ali with half-lidded eyes, take him places he'd never gone before with a woman. Not like this. Not this potent and heady and downright sexy.

Ali unleashed her passion and rode him with frenzy. She pleaded and moaned with ahs of sheer breathless delight. Oh God, he'd never seen anything so humanly beautiful.

Joe knew this was it—their last time tonight. There wasn't anything more they could possibly do to each other. They were spent and sated, and so when Ali climbed high, Joe met her there and they shattered together, in unison crying out each other's names.

Ali stayed atop him a minute, looking at him with eyes that were unreadable. Then she climbed off, breaking their connection and lay beside him. Immediately, he wound her in his arms and held her. "That was the best sex of my life, Ali. I'm the luckiest man alive."

With that, Ali burst into tears.

Ali bounded out of bed, her heart broken. Unstoppable tears streamed down her face. She couldn't do this anymore. She hated lying to Joe, and the guilt ate at her each day.

She shoved her arms into her silk robe and walked over to the window, her body wracked with anguish. She hugged her middle tight.

"Ali, Ali, what is it?" Joe came up behind her. He put his arms onto her shoulders. "What have I done to upset you?"

Ali whipped around to face him, wiping her tears with the back of her hands. "Nothing, Joe. You haven't done a thing. It's me. I'm the guilty one here."

Ali moved away from Joe, breaking off all contact. She

put the middle of the room between them. She hated seeing the look of puzzlement on Joe's face. "It's just that I can't do this to you anymore."

"Do what, honey?" he asked, softly, being gentle with her. She was probably confusing the hell out of him.

"I'm not the person you think I am. I'm certainly not the soft-spoken, passive little woman I've been pretending to be since almost the minute you hired me back here. I don't like wearing pencil skirts and business suits and putting my hair up in buns. I don't even *need* glasses. Those are fakes. I always wear contacts."

Joe slipped into his briefs and put on his glasses at the mention of hers. He shook his head. "What's going on, Ali, really?"

"Really? *Really?* I'm in love with you. I mean, the Real Ali is, but you didn't notice her, with her sassy mouth and trendy clothes and flamboyant nature. The whole time when we worked together in New York, you never looked at me as anything but your employee. If my hair caught on fire, you wouldn't have noticed me. And then you kissed me goodbye at the airport, and I knew there could be something great between us."

"It was a great kiss, Ali. But I wasn't looking—"

"I know all about it. I know about Sheila what's-her-name and how she broke your heart. I know you didn't want an office romance and boy, you sure as hell stuck to your guns." Ali softened her voice, "But then you called and asked me to work for you, and I came. I flew across the continent to work for you, Joe."

"Ali, where is this going?"

She shuddered and her nerves went raw. "I'm trying to tell you. You wouldn't notice the Real Ali, so I made up Fake Ali. I changed my whole personality to get your attention. You see, what we have now isn't real. Nothing about me is real."

Joe pointed to the bed. "That's as real as it gets, Ali."

"Yes, that was real. But all those other times, I held back—afraid to show you who I was."

A storm brewed in Joe's dark eyes. "I knew it. I sensed that something was wrong. The question is why the hell you thought you had to deceive me."

Tears pooled in her eyes. "I guess I was desperate to have you any way I could." Ali took a breath to steady her nerves. There was no going back now. She had to own up to all of it. "Tonight I opened up and showed you the real me. I couldn't go through with it anymore. I feel so bad about this, Joe."

He remained quiet, as if trying to absorb her confession.

"I don't want you to fall for a woman who is a fraud. That's what I am, a fraud."

"Noble of you to admit it, Ali." She didn't miss the sarcasm in his voice.

"I've been acting all this time. And I can't do it anymore. I'm sorry, Joe."

More tears spilled down her cheeks. She reached for a tissue and hastily wiped them away. "I'm bold and opinionated, and I say what's on my mind. Men notice me. They want me. But not you, Joe. You never wanted the real me."

"You're blaming me for your deception?"

"No, I'm taking all the blame. It's all my fault."

Finally what she told him began sinking in. He pushed his glasses back and forth on his nose and then shook his head, casting her a look of disdain. "Then what Sheila told me about you was true."

"Sheila?" Ali's heart stopped in that instant. "What, how…"

"In San Francisco. She warned me about you. She told me about your mother—her five husbands and all the men in between. She warned me that you were playing me. I didn't take her seriously. But my curiosity got the better of me. I looked Justine Holcomb up. It's amazing what a person can find out on the Internet."

"You investigated me?" Ali's temper skyrocketed.

"Not you but your mother."

"And what did you find, Joe?" She put her hands on her hips, defying him to answer, while inside her heart was breaking.

"A lot, Ali. Your mother has quite a reputation for her conquests. She did just about anything she could to get a ring on her finger. Oh, I didn't want to believe it. But you," he said, his voice thick with accusation, "you're just like her. You manipulated me, Ali. Admit it."

"You're confusing me with Sheila. She's the one who burned you. And she had the nerve to warn you about *me?*" Ali's shackles rose. The hairs on her arms stood on end.

Joe approached her, his voice firm and filled with disgust. "Sheila isn't the issue here. You are. You knew all along that you were deceiving me, acting out a role to what? String me along?"

"No!"

"Get your hands on my money?"

"No!"

"Blow my mind with sex, so I wouldn't catch on."

She slapped his face.

Joe grabbed her hand and stared at her. Through tight lips, his voice cold and hard, he looked deep into her eyes. "I never wanted to believe it of you, Ali. But it's all clear now. Your clothes, your personality, you changed it all to fool me. Hell, you even changed your bedroom habits. Your mother taught you well."

He dismissed her, just like that. He grabbed his clothes, slipping into his pants quickly, and walked out of her bedroom without a second glance.

She jumped when she heard the front door slam. And burst into tears for the second time tonight.

Tumultuous emotions roiled in Joe's gut. He walked at a fast pace, trying to burn off some of his anger and despair. He'd sent the limo home, thinking he'd be with Ali until the morning. So now he found himself furious, barefoot and half dressed walking down the highway toward home.

It had been on the tip of his tongue to tell Ali he was in love with her. That would have made her charade complete, he thought with disgust.

She'd already made a colossal fool of him.

Yes, he'd noticed changes in her, but who could figure a woman's mind? Joe thought Ali had been a little more contemplative lately due to the newness of her surroundings. Maybe she'd felt out of her element and needed time to acclimate to California living. She had few friends here, and all that combined could have an effect on a woman.

But Ali hadn't felt any of those things. No, she'd simply had one goal in mind—to trick him into a relationship.

She was just like her mother.

Joe had read accounts of how Justine Holcomb left her first husband for a wealthy oilman. Then a few years later, she'd become a caregiver for an ailing supermarket mogul and had divorced husband number two and moved on to husband number three. She had ties to famous male actors, real estate tycoons and clothing designers. More husbands, more boyfriends, the list went on and on. No wonder Ali never wanted to talk about her family. Speaking of it would have tipped her hand.

After Joe's fury subsided a little, he pressed Nick's number on his iPhone. The phone rang several times. "I hope I'm interrupting," Joe grumbled after his brother finally answered.

"What?" Nick sounded flustered. "Joe, is that you? Do you know what time it is? Like two in the morning."

"Early for you. I need a ride."

"Now? What the hell. Can't you call—"

"No, I'm in no mood to explain myself. Just pick me up. And don't keep me waiting." Joe gave him the location and plopped himself down by the side of the road.

Ten minutes later, Nick showed up in his red Ferrari, and Joe got in. "You look like crap, man. Have a fight with Ali?"

"More than a fight. Just take me home, Nick, and don't ask any questions."

Nick cast him a concerned look and didn't offer up any snarky remarks, for which Joe was grateful.

When he got home, he emptied half a bottle of Scotch, drank himself into oblivion, replaying his argument with Ali in his head until he couldn't think anymore. He fell into bed and slept off the effects of the alcohol.

In the morning, he frowned at the clock by his bedside when he saw the time. He'd slept past noon and rose with a splitting headache. Apparently, he hadn't slept off all the liquor he'd consumed. He felt like hell.

He lumbered downstairs for a cup of coffee and found *both* brothers sitting in the kitchen. Tony was here? And Rena, too? They all gazed at him with sympathetic eyes.

He whipped around abruptly to walk away. The quick movement brought pain to his skull. He rubbed his head.

"Sit down, Joe," Nick called to him.

"I'm bad company today," he muttered.

"I'll get you a cup of coffee," Rena said, her voice hopeful.

He turned, and she sent him a sweet look. He could easily blow off his brothers, but his sister-in-law deserved better treatment. "Thanks."

Rena was already up and pouring his coffee. She brought it to him and gestured for him to take a seat at the table. He hesitated a second, then sank down in the seat. He directed his attention to Tony. "What are you doing here?"

"It was my idea to come over," Rena said. "I was hoping you'd come down while we were here."

"Yeah, why?"

"Because, um," Rena began, looking guilty about something. "I know what happened between you and Ali."

"You *know?*" Joe sipped his steamy coffee while holding his head steady. "News travels fast."

"Ali called me this morning. She's very upset."

Joe gave a slight nod. "She should be."

Rena leaned back in her seat and sighed deeply. "Oh, believe me, she is."

"If you ask me, having a woman that amazing go to such great lengths to get you to notice her ain't the worst thing that could happen, man," Nick said. "You've got rocks in that geek brain of yours if you haven't figured that out yet."

"I didn't ask you." Joe sent his brother a grim look.

Nick glanced at Tony, who in turn glanced at Rena. His sister-in-law put her hand on her growing belly, and Joe was reminded to tread carefully with her.

"Joe, she really cares about you," Rena said.

"Until the next sucker comes along." This time he took a big swallow of his coffee and burnt his tongue. "Damn it."

"I think you should hear her out," Rena said quietly.

"If you know what she did, then how can you ask that of me? She's a phony. Just like her mother."

"Oh, Joe," Rena said, nibbling on her lower lip. She glanced at Tony, who sent her a nod of encouragement. "What if I told you I had a hand in that little scheme?"

"I'd say no one forced Ali to follow through with it. You probably thought you were helping. She knew better."

"The last thing Ali wants is to be like her mother. Perhaps you've judged her too harshly."

"I've been burned before, remember?"

Rena flinched. "I know, Joe. But Ali seemed so perfect..."

Joe rose. "Thanks for stopping by. I'll live."

He left the three of them and walked out of the kitchen and up the stairs. At least he had a day to get Ali out of his system—until he had to face her at work tomorrow.

Ali called in sick on Monday. It was the first time she hadn't come to work since Joe had met her. On Tuesday, he walked into his office and stopped short when he spotted a young blond woman sitting at Ali's desk.

He approached her with furrowed brows. "Who are you?"

She smiled wide, showing sparkling white teeth. "I'm Georgia Scott, from the Short Notice temporary agency." She rose from behind Ali's desk and put out her hand. "You must be Mr. Carlino."

"Joe Carlino," he said, still trying to figure this out. He shook her hand absently. "Where's Ali, Ms. Pendrake?"

"I don't know. Ms. Pendrake called our office yesterday and said you needed a temp. That would be me. She faxed me very detailed instructions." The woman lifted up several sheets of handwritten papers.

Joe nodded, unnerved seeing Ali's desk occupied by someone else. "Did she say how long you'd be here?"

The woman shot him a quizzical look. "At least two weeks."

Joe entered his office and listened to his messages. He had four, and the last one was a breathless Ali.

"Hello, Joe. Under the circumstances, it would be best if I didn't work for you anymore. I know you think the worst of me, and I'm not going to beg you for forgiveness. I made a mistake, and I'm truly sorry. I've arranged for a temp and hope she works out until you can find a suitable replacement for me. You'll have my official resignation on your desk tomorrow. If I'm nothing else, I'm efficient." She laughed sadly into the phone before the message ended.

Joe stared at the answering machine for several minutes, feeling a hollow sense of loss.

And that feeling persisted the rest of the week. He'd made several attempts to call Ali, but his pride had him clicking off before the phone could ring. What could he say to her? He didn't even know who Ali was anymore. It wasn't just that the hair, makeup and demeanor had changed but it was the entire idea behind it that galled him. Was she really that calculating and devious?

Made a man think what else she would have done to gain his attention.

By the middle of the next week, Joe dreaded coming into work each day and not seeing Ali behind her desk. He'd thought he'd get used to seeing Ms. Scott there, typing away, bringing him reports, making his appointments, but that surely didn't happen. Worse yet, he hadn't lapped his swimming pool since the day Ali quit her job. He'd lost his desire and found most mornings he dragged himself out of bed and forced himself to go to work. His well-ordered life had taken a nosedive.

This morning, as he walked into the front doors of Carlino Wines, noting that Georgia Scott wasn't at her desk, Joe's mood lifted a little. He'd come to resent the woman who wasn't Ali. Yet as he approached his own office, he slowed when he reached the doorway. His heart rate sped, and hope that he never thought he'd feel again surged forth. Ali sat in his office. Her back was to him, and she sat erect, holding her head up high, her beautiful long auburn hair flowing in curls down her back.

He entered quietly. "Ali?"

The woman turned her head and looked at Joe with stunning jade-green eyes. She smiled Ali's smile, but she wasn't Ali. "I'm Justine Holcomb, Ali's mother. You must be Joe."

Shocked by the resemblance, Joe took a second before acknowledging her. "Yes, Joe Carlino."

She put out her hand, and Joe took it, giving a gentle shake. "Please, if I may have a minute of your time. I came a long distance to speak with you."

Her soft, gentle voice surprised him. She didn't sound like Ali, but she sure as hell looked like her—a slightly older version but Justine Holcomb was every bit as beautiful as Ali.

"Of course." Joe took a seat at his desk and waited.

"I can see why Ali loves you," she began, not mincing words. "And by the hope in your eyes before you realized I wasn't Ali, I think you feel the same way."

"If you came all this way, to tell me how I feel—"

"No, Joe. I didn't. I came to tell you how *I* feel."

And Justine Holcomb poured out her heart to him, explaining how she'd grown up poor and wanted so much from life. She told him how her becoming a beauty queen might have been the worst thing that could have happened to her. That she floundered in relationships, never being satisfied, always looking for something that she could never quite attain.

"I wasn't a very good role model for my daughter. Lord knows, I've finally come to realize that now, in my older years. I'm extremely proud of Ali, Joe. Unlike me, she knows what she wants in life. She's decisive and smart, and she's never wanted to climb social ladders. Believe me when I tell you it's the very last thing on her mind. I know she fears living the same kind of life I've led. She's done everything in her power *not* to be like me, but I know she wants love in her life, Joe. She wants a home and a family."

Joe didn't know what to say to that.

She watched him with assessing eyes. "I see you're thinking this through. That's good. Don't make snap judgments. I've done that all my life, and look where that got me? Finally, after five husbands, I've found true happiness, and it took a near-fatal heart attack for me to see how much I love my husband. Ali's smarter than me. She only wants one good man in her life."

He let go a deep pent-up breath.

"And if you don't believe that and think she's just like me, let me share this with you. Since leaving your employ, she's been approached by two of your most formidable competitors to come work for them. Both have offered her great opportunities with more money and frills than she received working for you, if I might add. Ali turned them both down. My daughter is beautiful, and if I might say, she could have her choice of a dozen rich wealthy men, if that were her goal. She doesn't want that—or them. She only wants you."

Justine rose from her seat and smiled. "Think about it, Joe. Think about Ali and what she really means to you."

Joe stood up. "I will. Thank you for coming by. I know it wasn't easy for you."

"Oh, but it was. For my daughter, I'd do anything. I have a lot of making up to do where Ali is concerned." She cast him a sad smile. "Don't wait too long, Joe. Ali plans on moving back to the East Coast."

And with that, Justine turned and left, again with her head held high.

Joe shuddered as he watched her go.

"I knew that guy was a jerk," Royce said, helping Ali move some heavy boxes into her living room. The movers were coming tomorrow. It had been two weeks since she'd seen Joe on the best and worst night of her life. Two weeks and he hadn't called. Apparently his mind was made up.

"He's not a jerk," Ali said in Joe's defense. "He's just, well, I don't know what he is, but he's not a jerk."

Royce grumbled a reply, but Ali wasn't listening. She focused on her move back to New York. A teeny, tiny part of her thought she should confront Joe and talk it through with him before she left Napa for good, but Ali wasn't sure she could take another rejection from him. The past two weeks had been nightmarish for her. She'd spent all of her tears and had moved on to self-recriminations. She was angry with Joe, but she was even angrier with herself. She should have never concocted that scheme, yet her real anguish came each minute of every day when she realized that they weren't meant for each other.

He doesn't want the real you.

After Royce left to go to work late in the morning, Ali kept busy packing up boxes with her clothes and kitchen items. At noon, when her doorbell rang, she called out, "Coming," and grabbed her wallet for the pizza she'd ordered.

"How much do I owe you?" she asked, opening the door and fumbling with her cash.

"Not a thing. I owe you."

A sharp gasp escaped when Ali recognized Joe's deep voice.

He stood on her threshold, dressed in blue jeans and a black polo shirt, looking more delicious than hot fudge melting over a mound of rich vanilla ice cream.

He smiled, and his dark eyes gleamed; Ali thought she'd be melting soon. "What are you doing here?"

Joe peered over her shoulder, taking note of the boxes she had stacked up. "I owe you two things, Ali. The first one is an apology. I wasn't happy with you the other day. In fact, I was disappointed and well, pissed. No one likes to be made a fool."

"Joe, I said I was sorry. It was a big mistake," she implored. At the very least she wanted him to know she regretted how she'd tried to trick him.

"I know, Ali. But I shouldn't have reacted that way. I didn't let you explain. Instead, I assumed the worst about you. I shouldn't have said those things about your mother, either. She's actually a very honest woman."

Ali put her hands on her hips and ignored the hope that filled her heart. "And you know this how?"

"We spoke."

"You spoke...on the phone? Did my mother call you?" Ali's heart raced.

Oh, God, Mom, what did you do?

"No, she didn't call me. She came to see me. Yesterday. She gave me a lot to think about."

"She was here? In Napa? I didn't know," she said, shocked and fearful of how that encounter went. "I didn't put her up to it, Joe. You have to believe me. I understand how you feel about me. I know we're incompatible. We're different as night and day and you don't want—"

Joe leaned close and put two fingers to her lips. "Shh, Ali." His touch caused a quake to rumble through her body. "You don't know how I feel."

When Joe removed his fingers, she opened her mouth to reply, then clamped it shut.

"I said I owed you two things. The first one is my apology. And I hope you accept it."

Ali nodded. "I do."

"And the second one is our bike tour. I regret not following through on that. I owed you that much for all your help, and I keep my promises."

Her heart could have been swept aside with a broom. All the hope she didn't dare count on faded to nothingness. "It's okay, Joe. As you can see, I'm moving. I don't need to see Napa anymore."

"But you do. At least let me take you to one place that's very special to me." Joe moved away from her door so she could see the two touring bikes with helmets on the seats, waiting for them.

Ali furrowed her brows. He seemed so adamant, and what did she have to lose? At least, maybe the two of them could wind up as friends. Okay, maybe not friends. But they could end their relationship on a better note. It would just about kill her to be with him today, but Ali had always been a fool when it came to Joe.

"Fine. I'll put my tennis shoes on."

And five minutes later, Ali, dressed in her moving clothes, a tank top, workout pants and a slick red-striped helmet followed Joe down the highway. It was a road she'd seen a zillion times. An occasional car whizzed by them, and Joe looked back to make sure she was okay. They'd gotten only a few miles from her condo, when Joe pulled off the road by a white wooden fence that separated two properties. Green grass, with vineyards in the distance, sloped down to a little clearing. There, Ali saw a blanket laid out, with champagne cooling in a bucket and flowers set in a little vase.

Joe removed his helmet and got off his bike. Ali did the same. He approached and led her to the blanket just a few feet off the road. "Joe? What is this?"

"It's the only stop on our bike tour, Ali. Come, have a seat."

Joe waited for her to sit on the blanket and then he took a place next to her. Ali looked out, but all she saw was the road ahead of them and vineyards in the background. Confused, she shook her head. "I don't get it."

Joe took her hand, and a jolt of electricity coursed between them. Ali knew it wasn't one-sided. She could tell by the gleam in Joe's eyes that he felt it, too. "Neither did I for a long time. After our fight the other night—"

"You mean, the night you walked out on me after we nearly burned up the sheets in bed?"

Joe appeared chagrined. "Yeah, that night. I walked and walked and thought. I was angry and hurt. And all sorts of things entered my mind. But the one thing that kept coming back to me, over and over again, was that I was so angry with you because I'd fallen in love with you. It was here, right here, as I waited for Nick to pick me up, that I figured it all out. I was ready to tell you that night, but then…"

"I blew it," Ali said softly.

Joe squeezed her hand. "I was burned really badly with Sheila, and I didn't want to even consider another relationship, much less one with my very best personal assistant. Maybe, I'd been a little obtuse about it."

"You think?" Ali said with a grin, her whole world looking much brighter now.

"Yeah, but I'd always liked you. Maybe too much. That's why I couldn't bring myself to fall for you. I held back, but if you think I didn't notice you, you're dead wrong. I noticed. How could I not? You're smart and fun and gorgeous, Ali. I noticed it all. But I was protecting myself. It wasn't so much that *you'd* changed that drew me to you. It was that *I'd* changed. I was ready to give us a chance, finally. It took me a long time, I know. So sue me. I'm slow on the uptake."

"You make up for it, though. In bed." Ali smiled sweetly, and Joe's eyes widened. Then he chuckled.

"Ali, I don't think I can live without you. You and I are like night and day, but who said that's a bad thing? Opposites attract, sweetheart. And life would never be boring. I love you, Ali Pendrake. Marry me. Be my wife, the mother of my children and please," he pleaded, "come back to work for me."

Ali threw her head back and laughed, her heart filling with joy. "I want a raise."

"You got it."

"And a house of our own."

"You got that, too."

"And children, right away. I'm not getting any younger."

"Right away?" Joe cast her such a loving smile that her nerves tingled. "I'm for that."

"I love you, Joe. With all my heart."

Joe leaned over and brushed a soft kiss to her lips. "I love you, Ali. Just the way you are."

Ali's heart warmed, believing that her mother had finally come through for her this time, and that compounded her joy.

Joe poured champagne, and they toasted to new beginnings. Cars continued to whiz by, but Ali sat back on the blanket off the side of the road in Napa Valley and thought it was the most romantic proposal a woman could ever hope to receive.

* * * * *

Don't miss the
exciting conclusion of the
NAPA VALLEY VOWS *miniseries*
The Billionaire's Baby Arrangement,
available in August
from Silhouette.

Five hunky Texas single fathers—five stories from Cathy Gillen Thacker's LONE STAR DADS *miniseries. Here's an excerpt from the latest, THE MOMMY PROPOSAL from Harlequin American Romance.*

"I hear you work miracles," Nate Hutchinson drawled. Brooke Mitchell had just stepped into his lavishly appointed office in downtown Fort Worth, Texas.

"Sometimes, I do." Brooke smiled and took the sexy financier's hand in hers, shook it briefly.

"Good." Nate looked her straight in the eye. "Because I'm in need of a home makeover—fast. The son of an old friend is coming to live with me."

She was still tingling from the feel of his warm palm. "Temporarily or permanently?"

"If all goes according to plan, I'll adopt Landry by summer's end."

Brooke had heard the founder of Nate Hutchinson Financial Services was eligible, wealthy and generous to a fault. She hadn't known he was in the market for a family, but she supposed she shouldn't be surprised. But Brooke had figured a man as successful and handsome as Nate would want one the old-fashioned way. *Not that this was any of her business...*

"So what's the child like?" she asked crisply, trying not to think how the marine-blue of Nate's dress shirt deepened the hue of his eyes.

"I don't know." Nate took a seat behind his massive antique mahogany desk. He relaxed against the smooth leather of the chair. "I've never met him."

"Yet you've invited this kid to live with you permanently?"

"It's complicated. But I'm sure it's going to be fine."

Obviously Nate Hutchinson knew as little about teenage

HAREXP0810

boys as he did about decorating. But that wasn't her problem. Finding a way to do the assignment without getting the least bit emotionally involved was.

Find out how a young boy brings Nate and Brooke together in THE MOMMY PROPOSAL, coming August 2010 from Harlequin American Romance.

HAREXP0810